the
ADVENTURE
of
GILBERT CASANOVA

The Adventure of
Gilbert Casanova

Colin O'Brien

For more information, email:

ColinOBrienBooks@gmail.com

ISBN: 979-8-9876506-0-8

Cover designed by Colin O'Brien

10 9 8 7 6 5 4 3 2

FIRST EDITION

To Jim and Ann

Contents

This Page Left Blank

Part 1
The Queen of Zane

November 24, 2021

1 ... The Fool from Tennessee

The outlandish exuberance and overall snobbery of high society left a bitter taste in Gilbert Casanova's mouth. No one was ever who they said they were. He spit caviar back in its cup and focused on the fresh wave of beautiful, sinister guests descending to the ballroom.

Even at a distance he caught himself disarmed by the tailored suits and practiced smiles. He was used to slavers and traders, not prims and propers. Most were double, even triple his age. Finding the man was trickier than expected. Maybe he was looking at it the wrong way?

He motioned to a server.

"Did you change your mind?" she asked. "Pots at fifteen hundred. Bets locked in three. Front runners are a fella' from Texas and them Europeans – yellow dress, leopard shawl – they were seen arguing."

Gilbert weighed his options. He was convinced the young man with the pink flower would cause the biggest scene. The wife, or who he assumed was the wife, seemed unnaturally ticked.

"Sir?"

To hell with it.

"Pink feather," Gilbert dug into his pocket and pulled out a wad of cash. "What about the other bit?"

"Miss Bronte is due to arrive in seven. I haven't noticed anything odd, but my eyes…"

He slipped her a twenty dollar bill.

She raised an eyebrow.

Another twenty.

"Oh come on, that's plenty."

"Hmph. Is there anything else?"

"Water, please, when you have a chance. And is there a trashcan nearby?"

She took the cup and left.

He pulled at the suffocating black turtleneck and let his eyes wander. Pale, wrinkled men clutched girls more plastic than flesh. Royalty forced laughter. Young millionaires huddled to-gether between carved gold columns depicting the fall of Lucifer. More guests poured down the grand staircase, pointing at the painted family tree growing from slabbed marble to mirrored ceiling. He counted one hundred and five small white circular tables packed around an empty dance floor. The place reeked of southern culture. Old southern culture. Their host, the Honorable Reginald R. R. Robertson, gushed over how many centuries the house and land had been in his family. With faked interest Gilbert listened to the endless contributions each name gave to God and country until he was forced to excuse himself.

Focus. Maybe it wasn't as simple as a tattoo or ring. Surely one doesn't just ask if the other was part of a secret society.

The band started to play, and his attention was drawn to the top of the stairs. Holy…no. Yes. How? Damn. For a moment he forgot who he was looking at.

Angela Bronte's dress shimmered like liquid gold inlayed with a billion diamonds. Brown stones on silver threads traced the lines of her arms and hands. Around her neck and waist looped an hourglass of sapphires that fell against her bare stom-ach and a thick violet shawl covered her back.

Every eye watched the mysterious beauty descend from heav-en. He tried to guess the stories they gave her. A noble's daughter with a taste for danger? A rich heiress looking for her newest toy? A mere nobody who scraped just enough money in hopes of finding a gilded future before time took its toll?

One by one men downed their drinks and left their parties. He felt the slightest daggers of jealousy and revulsion.

The server returned with his water. And champagne.

"Appreciate it, but I'm afraid I didn't order this."

"It's a gift, sir. A lady wishes to speak with you."

"Please tell her thank you, but I'll pass."

There was no reply.

Something hard pressed into his back.

"Move and you're dead."

2 ... Old Friends

Gilbert slowly turned.

The woman, late twenties, was an Egyptian with a strong jaw and simple cream-colored dress. Black hair fell along her shoulders.

"Gilbert Casanova," white teeth flashed between red lips, "if this was a real gun, you'd be dead right now."

"Listening and thinking never were my best qualities. Always a pleasure, Caroline. Hardly recognized you in that dress. Who is it this time? Senator? Athlete? Movie star?"

"King," she held up her hand to reveal a large black and gold diamond. "Dreadfully old, dreadfully boring, dreadfully rich.

The wedding was marvelous. Camels, elephants, music for miles."

"I'll be sure to send a gift. You look good, by the way."

"Not bad yourself. But you do know this is black-tie?"

"You know me." He sipped his water. It sounded better in his head.

"Yes. Which makes me wonder, why exactly are you here?"

Before he could answer a man as tall and dark as an olive branch with hair just as greasy appeared by her side. Numerous medals swung on a jacket for acts Gilbert assumed never happened.

"My love, what have I told you about talking to the help? I kid. I kid." The man wrapped his arm around his wife. "Are you enjoying yourself Mister…?"

"Canyon," she said, "Mister Canyon was just telling me how sad it was his husband couldn't make it. Stomach bug, you said?"

"Yes. Horrible timing."

The man's face relaxed and a short laugh escaped. "Such a shame. What do you do for work, Mister Canyon?"

"Purveyor of rare antiquities."

"Like an art collector?"

"In a way. More so an adventurer."

"I see. Have you two met before?"

"Caroline and I crossed paths in Colombia a few months ago. Kept in touch for a little bit, but life gets in the way."

"Small world, isn't it? Well, I would love to stay and chat, but I hear someone calling for me."

No one was.

Gilbert nodded and waited for the king to disappear back into the crowd.

Caroline smiled innocently. "Oh, it's just a bit of fun. These things get so dull and he gets so worked up at the smallest bits. It's just— Forgive me. Here I am rambling."

Never change, Caroline.

"Anyways, why are you here? You wouldn't happen to be purveying anything, would you? Not that the options are limited."

"Friends with the host and got the invite. I was actually getting ready to leave before you jumped me." His eyes caught Angela surrounded by a number of men.

"Recognize someone?"

"No. Just looked familiar."

Caroline's face narrowed. "It is quite a funny coincidence, running into you here."

"I know, right. These parties aren't exactly my style."

"Not that. It's…the last I heard, you were still fighting for the Butcher down in Peru. And had all your fingers."

The name made Gilbert's spine curl. "I appreciate the concern, but he let me go. Made good on our agreement."

"That's a first." A dangerous look grew on her face. "We should celebrate." She snapped her fingers. "You there! Bring us that champagne." She handed him a glass and raised her voice. "To Gilbert Casanova. Adventurer."

Gilbert put the glass to his lips but didn't drink. Already rumors swirled. An adventurer? Here? How delicious.

A lady joined them. "Excuse me. I couldn't help but hear something about Peru. Have you been? I've always wanted to go, but you know how it is."

Two more appeared. "Do you have any stories?"

"I've been on plenty of cruises," said a man.

A small audience formed.

Caroline smiled devilishly. "Go on, mister adventurer, tell us a tale."

One story couldn't hurt. "Well, one time I worked out west as a cowboy."

3 ... Our Little Secret

For the next hour Gilbert dazzled with stories of daring escapes
and exaggerated bravery. The growing crowd loved it. He loved
it. They hung on his every word.

"...and in my infinite wisdom I let the beast go, thinking surely she wouldn't run. Well, I close the gate and she begins to
wander. I start following, and before I know it, I'm hanging off
the back of the saddle while she's galloping into the forest. Sand
and dirt are flying through the air—"

His heel erupted in pain.

"I am so sorry! It's these shoes. They're absolutely awful."
Emerald eyes glared back at him. Angela was even more beauti-

ful up close. "Now, just who do we have here? Quite the little celebrity, aren't you?"

He smiled. "Quite alright, madame. Gilbert Casanova. Adventurer."

"Adventurer? Really? I would never expect to see an adventurer at a party like this. Especially one with such a strict dress code. And planning. And importance. And planning. But what do I know?"

Perfume stung his eyes. There was no turning back. He took up a shovel and continued digging himself deeper. "Well, I was told classy. Not penguin."

"Told by whom?"

He coughed. "I don't believe I caught your name?"

A woman cut in. "Mister Casanova, this is Madame Silver, the daughter of Rykon Silver, the oil magnate." So heiress it was! Gilbert internally congratulated himself. "Madame, you must hear one of his stories. Tell her the one when you saved a child from those vicious slavers. Or the one when you fought pirates in Madagascar."

"Silver?" Surely it was just a coincidence. "What a pleasure."

"At your service. Charming, isn't it? Silver in gold." Jewels jingled as she did a little spin.

"It's a lovely dress on a lovely lady."

"Yes, I know it is." Her smile registered like a siren. "If you wouldn't mind, could I get your opinion on something? I adore history — gobble it all up — and there's this statue I was hoping you may know something about."

"Of course. Perhaps we could talk after the party?"

"Could you spare a moment right now while I have your attention? It'll only take a minute. If we could just step outside?"

"Lead the way." Gilbert made his apologies to the crowd and followed. His eyes darted to the stairs. Maybe he could make a run? Disappear amongst the tables?

The cool air bit his skin.

"What. In the Hell. Was that?" Angela stormed towards him, throwing her arm into his chest and driving him against the stone balcony. The jewels dug into his skin. "I thought the plan was ta keep a low profile? Not show ya face?"

"It was, but—"

"How do ya manage ta screw every damn part up, huh? Classy, Gilby. Class-y. Not school teacha' witha wardrobe. I mean, where did ya even get these clothes?" She paced back and forth. "And then ya get ova half the party ta watch ya tell stories? Ya saved a little kid? And ya name is Gilbert Casanova? Ya real name? Why?" Her fingers twisted as if strangling his soul. "Holy whores. I thought ya was smart." She raised a hand to silence him. "Then ya go and get all close ta the Queen of Zane?"

"You saw that?"

"Yes! Everyone saw it! Ya have any idea who she is? And her husband? This ain't some pub. This ain't some guy ya have a disagreement with, fight, and just move on. He's not nobody. Santa mierda. Now, ya either gonna leave or stay out here. I'm going back in ta flirt with a buncha' old money bags who thinks they can grab whatever they want just ta find out where this stupid key might be, which, ding ding, hello, I— we need. I'm the only one taking the hit. Do I make myself clear?" She threw on a smile and marched back inside.

Breathe. Focus. Breathe.

Gilbert chucked his empty glass into the greens and listened to it shatter. Idiot! How could he have been so stupid? They had a job to do, and he went and played hero.

"Someone's been keeping secrets."

Gilbert spun to see Caroline emerge from the shadows.

"Relax. My lips are sealed. It can be our little secret. Come, sit with me. It's terribly cold."

Gilbert remained as he was.

"Oh, don't go all stoic on me. It happens to the best of us. What's this about a key?"

He'd already said too much. "It's been a long day and I'm just gonna call it." He made for the door.

"Wait." She grabbed his arm with surprising strength. "No need to run off so early. I think we can help each other."

"Caroline, I—"

"You're still after Womack's treasure, aren't you? I happen to know where the key is."

His mouth went dry.

Her eyes glimmered like a shark.

Maybe he could salvage things.

Against his better judgement he took a seat. She came closer and took his hands. The icy grip felt off.

"Can I tell you a secret? I don't do all this for the money. I'm not that vain. I do it because if I don't, I'll die. Just like you fighting for the Butcher. You think marrying a man twice my age is fun? Last month he fathered a child with some peasant girl. He uses me like a rag." She went on detailing the tragedies of her life.

Gilbert wanted to believe her. If the conversation happened months earlier, he would've taken her hands and offered a word of comfort. A hug, even. But now…

"I'm sorry."

"Don't be. I'm rich. That makes up for it all, right?" she wiped her face. "How old are you, Gilbert? Thirty? Thirty-five?"

"Twenty-three."

"Twenty-three?" Her eyes widened in playful shock. "So mature. Such a gentleman. My birthday is actually next week. The big three-oh."

"Happy birthday," he said bluntly. Where was this going?

"In my country it's custom to give a kiss to celebrate. Like this," she leaned over and kissed him on the lips.

It felt wrong. The way she lingered. Tasting. Testing. She went for another.

He broke away and stood. "No. We can't."

"Come on. You know you want to."

"My partner. Your husband. The party."

"Forget about them. Focus on me."

"You mentioned the treasure. What do you know?"

"Later. Just listen to my voice."

He needed to leave.

"You seem nervous. So serious. You keep looking at the door. Don't worry. No one's coming, Butcher's boy."

His blood went cold. His ears started to ring, and the smell of mint slithered into his nose.

She whispered in his ear. "Oh, don't think I don't know. Don't take me for a fool. Everyone knows about the bounty on your head. All it would take is a phone call. And that exchange with the little devil? Come on. I know where your little key is." She ran her hand along his leg.

"Maybe we can come to another arrangement?"

"No."

Where was Angela? Where was anybody?

"Let me make it clear for you. I always get what I want. And afterwards, you'll get what you want. If not, well, I'll tell every hunter, hitman, criminal, and piece of scum this place offers that Gabrielle Silver has two soldiers looking for Womack's treasure."

"I'm not- we're not with- who?" He'd never heard that name before.

She cupped his cheek. "Stupid doesn't look good on you."

Part 2
The Butcher of La Guerra

November 6, 2021

(18 Days Earlier)

4 ... La Guerra, an Island Near Peru

God damnit Gustav.

Gilbert rolled through the street and into a wall of cheering villagers. He felt the cut beneath his left eye.

A knife. A knife? Dance around, make it look close, put on a show. That was the plan. That was the agreement. That was what the Butcher said. No one ever mentioned a knife.

"Maldito Americano," hissed his opponent.

Even without the weapon the tall Chilean proved a challenge. He matched Gilbert step for step and every punch felt like it could break stone. One mistake, one lapse of judgment, and it'd be over. Physically, the man was perfect. Size, speed, strength, brains. Once the gun sounded the man waited. He must've watched other fights, noticed Gilbert let his opponents tire themselves. Clever. And spot on. There was one weakness, though. Yes, the Chilean was gifted, but he wasn't ready.

Hitting a patched leather bag in the quiet of a barn is nothing compared to La Guerra after dark. The crowd is as much a part of the fight as the fighters. They kick, they spit, they get under one's skin. Gilbert was still recovering from a pair of broken ribs. And they hated a boring fight.

The man was bending. Becoming frantic. Desperate.

Gilbert dug his fingers into the earth. Almost there. Closer. Closer.

The Chilean made his move. Gilbert shot forward, jerking his arm through the air and throwing dust in the man's face. Glass and nails and wood ripped their backs as they wrestled for control. One moment the man was on top clawing Gilbert's stomach, then it was Gilbert sinking teeth into flesh, the metallic taste filling his mouth. He dodged a wild fist and countered.

Crack!

The Chilean collapsed. The crowd roared. The circle tightened.

The man scrabbled for Gilbert's eyes, his ears, his teeth, his hair. Anything. It didn't matter. Gilbert wouldn't lose this fight. Losing meant death. Again and again he brought his fists down, the twitching mass under him growing weaker, looser, further away.

"NO-VA! NO-VA! NO-VA!"

"Se acabó! Lo estás matando! You kill!"

"Finish it!"

He was a god. If he were to call down lightning, he was certain the skies would answer. When the sun fell below the horizon and the shops hid behind their iron bars and their steel wires and the children snuck across crumbling rooftops and the less glamorous traits of humanity made themselves known — yes. Yes! They worshipped him. They sang his name. They made him an idol. For ten minutes every night nothing else mattered. Not the Butcher. Not the past. Not even Womack's treasure. He'd pound his chest and howl, arms and face painted black like the devil's, the chanting crowd echoing into the darkness.

Gilbert stood and pulled the limp body up by the hair.

"Si?" he yelled.

"Si!"

"Si?"

"Si!"

He placed his other hand under the man's jaw and prepared to twist.

A low ringing and the smell of mint overwhelmed his senses. Words, faces, everything blurred. Gilbert let go of the Chilean and stared at the blood dripping from his knuckles. What was he doing? This wasn't him.

"And for the thirty-second night in a row," cried the announcer, "your champion: The Great Casa-nova!"

The vile grins of the crowd turned sour. Their yellow teeth and their yellow eyes and their yellow hearts were on full display. "Finish him!"

A young woman rushed out and fell besides the barely breathing Chilean.

"Miguel? Miguel? Despierta! Despierta!"

Gilbert took a step forward then stopped. What was he going to do? He wasn't a doctor. And she wouldn't take his help. Hell, the last time he tried ended with eight stitches in his shoulder. Ignoring the pats and praise he pushed through the crowd to the bar and headed straight for the bathroom. His ears continued ringing, but that awful smell was gone. He turned on the faucet.

Breathe. Focus. Breathe.

The creature in the mirror was hardly recognizable: bloodshot eyes, mangled hair, black markings, bleeding cuts. More monster than man. He winced as the steaming water hit his arm. The gray sink turned red.

Breathe. Focus. Breathe.

He dug the towel into his arm. He rubbed harder, faster. He could feel flesh being ripped away.

Breathe. Focus. Brea-

He vomited.

This was a mistake. Damn Gustav. Damn the island. Damn the whole adventure. It was supposed to be five fights. Five! Months of stumbling across South America chasing empty rumors. Where was the treasure? What did he have to show for it?

There was a knock at the door. "Senor. Everything alright?"

Gilbert answered in broken Spanish and focused on his breathing. It's okay. Just hold on. Just a few more days.

He looked again at the reflection with tears in his eyes.

5 ... The Old Man

The next morning, half asleep, Gilbert pulled his truck along the fence, parked, and set to work throwing hay. The silhouettes of two dozen horses slowly made their way across the field.

He scratched the massive jaws and continued down the line. "Hey Rocket. Or are you Laurel?" He checked the legs. "Nope. Morning Carroll."

Tabasco. Snow. Rodrigo. Papa. He counted off. Twenty-three. Where was Rabbit? He climbed the fence and searched the field. There she was. Sleeping on her side. Gilbert let out a whistle. The horse's head shot up.

"Come on girl, breakfast time. You know that's not good for you."

Gilbert finished with the hay and headed to the barn. He kicked the door twice to scare off any rats or mice that spent the night. Disgusting creatures. He listened and, hearing nothing, opened it. The smell of stale manure and old leather greeted him. He threw his bag on the couch and walked past the wall of saddles and bags of feed to the back where they kept the generator. Four hard pulls and a puff of smoke later the tiny machine sputtered to life. Lights came on.

"About time you showed up," the old man leaned against the door frame and spat on the ground. Already his arms were covered in mud. "It's five-seventeen. You should've been here an hour ago."

"I know. I know." Gilbert pulled the box of leads down. "Had a fight last night."

"Oh, he knows. He always knows. No respect. This whole generation…" The old man shuffled over to the couch. "Back when I was a boy, let me tell ya…"

It was too early for a lecture. If there was any truth in the old man's words then back in his day people could lift mountains with one hand and run thirty miles in five minutes.

"Are you listening to me?"

"Yes." Gilbert looped the ropes around his arm and hurried outside.

"Do you know who you're getting?"

He hurried back and checked the list of names. Donny. Rev. Pluto. Javier. Bullseye.

"Slow. Slow. Don't rush it, they're not machines."

"Would help if I had some extra hands."

"Sure it would, and it would help if my body didn't hurt and I had better company that didn't complain and showed up on time. Tough shit."

The sky changed from red to orange to pink to blue and the short grasslands took form. It was a fine morning. While he brought the horses in and hooked them to their posts the old man filled bags with oats and began the daily inspections. The calm air and the smell of the ocean seemed to keep the beasts tame enough that , at least for the moment, life was enjoyable.

Gilbert saddled Rev and brought out the bit. The horse's lips stretched trying to inhale the metal.

"She been cribbing again?"

"A little. I've been putting aji on the rails. Doesn't seem to be working, though. Stupid girl."

Gilbert patted her neck and moved to Pluto. Her ears shot back and eyes widened. The closer he came the more she pulled away.

"Quit being a diva."

He tried again.

Pop!

The rope snapped and she was off.

There was dry laughter behind him.

"Try to get her before she reaches town this time."

Gilbert swung himself onto Rev, clicked twice, and launched his heels into the beast's sides.

6 ... Pluto

There was something about riding that couldn't be replicated and no matter how many times Gilbert did, it never failed to bring a smile to his face. The power. The rhythm. Saddle to air, air to saddle. Wind and dirt flying past. Freedom. And while at any moment the animal could stop and throw him, he knew she wouldn't. He squeezed his knees and held on.

The trail of dust took a sharp right towards the fields just outside of La Guerra. He pulled back on the reins and slowed twenty yards from Pluto. The horse glanced at them and went back to eating.

"Please don't run. Make it easy for me now." He inched forwards, freezing at the slightest twitch. "Come on girl. It's me."

He reached out and rubbed her jaw. "See. You're good. Not gonna hurt you. That's it. It's okay. You're alright, you pain in the ass." He clipped a rope to her lead. Gilbert gave a tug and Pluto followed him back to Rev and they began the return.

Despite all the island's faults it was still a beautiful little place. Sure, roofs were usually just painted aluminum and walls were either made of tires or clay or missing entirely and the smell of fish stuck around like a fog so thick one could grab it, but the people didn't seem to mind. Mothers raised children. Fathers worked the sea or fields. Gustav's men enforced rules. Compared to America it was, at times, a nice change of pace. Current situation notwithstanding.

As Gilbert passed into the older parts of the island, he slowed but remained alert. Every few days a ship would dock and strange men would load large crates — live cargo according to the old man — far too big for pigs or hens and far too small for cattle or horses. The vagueness only made him more curious. The island didn't export livestock, or anything come to think of it. His thoughts were interrupted by a group of kids running towards him asking to pet the horses.

Twenty minutes later he passed through the gates of the ranch. The old man was on his porch, waiting.

"I thought I told you to stop her before she got to town."

Gilbert grabbed a metal chair. "I did."

"Not from what I hear. Beer?"

He passed. The sun shined directly in his eyes and warmed his face. "Should probably start cleaning the barrels."

"What's this 'we' business?" The old man waved his hand. "They ain't going anywhere. You had a long night. Relax a minute. Tell me about the fight."

"Tall, thin, decent reach. Killer left jab. Kept going for my shoulder for some reason. Oh, and smart. Think he had a plan going in but wasn't ready for the crowd. Started acting weird. Lost his flow. Know if he had a wife or anything?"

"Why?"

"Some girl ran out after. Guy was in rough shape. Wanted to send flowers or money or something."

"No idea." The old man coughed from the back of his throat and spit. "Anything else happen?"

"Guy brought out a knife. Wasn't expecting that."

"Why not?"

"Why would I? It's not fair, and I know what you're going to sa—"

"Not fair?" The old man pulled himself up and shouted. "Do you hear that La Guerra? The great Gilbert Casanova thinks it wasn't fair." He sat back. "You're good kid, better than most Gustav sends my way, but thinking like that's gonna get you killed. Nearly did judging by that there cut. No one is thinking about fairness. If they did, I'd be on a beach with a case of beer and a couple señoritas. Instead, I'm drinking at seven o'clock on a mountain of horse shit and talking to you."

"Talking to me is like winning the lottery."

"Hmph. I'm so lucky."

Gilbert grinned and stretched. "Never really cared for the beach. Just sitting there's boring. Rather be up in the mountains. That or eating pizza."

"Pizza?"

"It's bread with tomato sauce and cheese and—"

"I know what pizza is, cojudo."

"Impossible to be unhappy eating a slice. Growing up my dad would take us to this place called Lorenzo's and order two large pies. Half-cheese, half-pepperoni, and half-sausage, half-banana peppers. I'm telling you, that pizza could cure cancer."

"My wife used to make one every Sunday."

"Never knew you were married."

"Aye. Darla. Eyes so blue it was like staring into the sky. Had a son named Pablo."

"What happened?"

"She wisened up and ran off with a better man. Oh well. But back to this whole fairness nonsense."

"I don't want to hurt anyone. Just do my job and be on my way."

"When you first showed up you said you wouldn't be here long. 'Five fights then I'm off to see Layla London'. Well, five fights go by. Then ten. Fifteen. Twenty. What are you up to now? Thirty-five? Thirty-six? I'm sure wherever you come from playing fair is the honorable thing and dirty is just that. But down here? With people like Gustav? Survival. Survival is what keeps you alive. The Butcher won't let a fighter walk, not when he's bringing in money. And don't give me that whole do my job speech. Son, I've seen your eyes light up when people call your name. You love it. Own it."

Gilbert shifted in his seat. Things hadn't gone exactly to plan, sure, but what choice did he have? Gustav's offer was the first lead in weeks. A roof, food, money, transportation…it was too good to pass up. "What's the end game? Honestly."

"Honestly? Well, honestly, you die. Or you're sold off to the highest bidder and then you die. Or even worse, you're sold off, don't die, are given a ranch and end up training more wide-eyed fools to keep the whole thing going. But until then there's work to do. Come on. Days-a-wasting."

For the rest of the morning and well into the evening they cleaned, trained, joked, and talked about life. Still, Gilbert's mind continued to return to the old man's words. Sold off? That had to be a joke. To who? Where? That was illegal.

When he locked the barn for the night a sheet of dark clouds were making their way from the west. Another uneventful day.

The old man hobbled over. "Don't think I forgot you showing up late." He tossed Gilbert a boat key. "The *Sin Timon*. First thing tomorrow. I want her spotless."

"You have a boat?"

"Won it off a drunk last week. Small dinky thing, but she floats. Now go. Vamos."

Gilbert got in his truck and left. As the car rumbled along he couldn't help but feel a little lucky. The last time he was late the old man made him run 10 miles and clear out the pasture. Cleaning a boat? Easy.

Gilbert parked behind the bar and went in through the back. He was ready for a shower and sleep. The stairs groaned with each step to the top floor. Hopefully the place wouldn't get too loud. He reached his door and stopped. A note was stapled to the wood.

SEE ME. - THE BUTCHER

7 ... Gustav the Butcher

Gilbert heard voices inside the room.

"Say that again. She wants what? Man! That's the funniest thing you've said all day. Whoo! Why should I care what that boss of yours wants? It's not her island. The only way she'll get it is from my cold dead hands," said Gustav.

"Is that an offer?" said the other.

Gilbert knocked and the room fell silent.

"That better be those little eggs I ordered!"

He recoiled at the strong odor of cigarettes and cheap liquor. The dark, overdecorated interior was filled with gaudy jewels and weapons and loud furniture. Green drapes matched a crunchy carpet. Sunk into the purple leather on the other side of a busy desk was the fat form of Gustav the Butcher. Gold chains rattled around his neck and stomach.

The other man — tall and muscular and visibly annoyed — leaned against a stack of black boxes with silver shields painted on the sides. Gilbert recognized the symbol from regular shipments but his knowledge ended there.

"There he is! Auriol," Gustav struggled to sit up, "this is the kid. This is the fighter I was telling you about, Gilbert Cassidy. Man, you should've seen him last night. He did it all. Put on a show for the town and put the other dude in coma. Best I've seen in years."

"Casanova. Wanted to see me?"

Auriol circled Gilbert, studying every inch like he were cattle. "Decent size. Nothing spectacular. Handsome enough. Age?"

"Twenty-one? He's in his early twenties."

"Room to grow. That cut looks fresh."

"You know how it is. The ring we use here is the road. Not that fluff you're used to. You worry too much my friend. Relax. Drink. Smoke. Don't overthink these things. He'll win."

"I'm not your friend, and you said the same thing about the last one. The kid didn't even make the ride over. If you're going to sell, we need them in one piece."

Sell? The familiar feeling of fear burrowed itself deep within Gilbert's throat and slithered down to his stomach. He started to cough.

Gustav waddled over and threw an arm around Gilbert. "This one. This one's the real deal. Close your eyes and I'll paint you a picture. Gold. Jewels. Sols as high as a New York City sky-scraper. But nah, that's not what your kind wants. You already have all that. What you really want, what you really need, is re-spect. And know what? I admire that. I love it! You want people to tremble when they say the name 'Silver.' You want them to shit themselves like an old lady. And this is the answer. He fights like he's possessed and man does he put on a show. The crowds will love him. They'll be screaming his name. And look, he's young," he pinched Gilbert's cheek, "not even in his prime. I'd say he's worth at least…oh…eighty-thousand."

"This whole island isn't worth eighty-thousand."

"Just a place to start. I'm open to negotiating."

"I'm not for sale," said Gilbert. The arm around his neck tightened.

"I watched the fight. He has potential but he's untrained. The fighters he'd see would kill him in ten seconds. You're in no po-sition to negotiate. Fifteen-thousand."

"I'm not for sale," Gilbert said louder.

"Fifteen? Fifteen? Man, you got some balls. What kind of an offer is that? Fifteen? I didn't know you were in the business of wasting people's time."

"Thirty-thousand. We paid fifteen for the last one."

"Fifty."

"We can do forty."

"Forty it is."

The two men shook hands.

Gilbert wriggled out from under the arm and backed away. His ears were ringing. His heart was racing. "Gustav, I've done my side of the deal. No more excuses. Where's London?"

"Funny, isn't he?" The butcher scratched his stomach and returned to his desk. "Do you want to take him tonight or tomorrow or when? Need to schedule fights, move things around, all that. Hey, aren't you from Dorado? How's your mama doing? Heard they have a witch problem. Some red headed coño." He lit another cigar.

"Tomorrow. Gustav, this one better be good. You said the same thing about the last one. And the one before that. And the one before—"

"Shush. Look. I'll admit, the last few have been rather messy, but that's not on me. Besides, this one's different. I can feel it. I got a thing for that."

"Mother's getting tired. Can you feel that?"

Gustav snorted. "Cultish freaks. 'Mother'. Know what? Your Madame Silver doesn't scare me. I bet I could get ten of my men, take a little cruise up to that island of yours, and beat the living piss out of every last one of you. A woman? Man you should be embarrassed! Whoo! The day I fear a woman — let me tell you — the day The Butcher fears a freaking woman is the day I lose all my senses. Man! The only reason she runs that operation is because she poisoned Rykon, and that's not a surprise. He always was a bad leader. Hey, and from what I hear, she's fallen off since that daughter of her's disappeared. Can't even get her kid to do something right. Know what, maybe I will pay a little visit. How's that sound?"

Auriol straightened to his full height. "I'll assume you're not thinking straight on account of it being late and the drinks from earlier. Insult Mother again and it will be the last thing you ever do. Now, as for payment—"

Gustav waved his hand for silence. "Really? You come to my home — my island — and threaten me? I love this. I love the confidence! Don't you love the confidence, Cassidy? Nah. That's not how this works. I thought all you Silvers were supposed to have brains or something."

"Relatively speaking, yes."

"Relatively speaking? Man! And he keeps the jokes coming. Feel proud of that one? Insult me then crack a joke?" Gustav shot out of the chair, grabbed Gilbert's hand, and slammed it on the table. "Let me show you something. This. This is what happens when people think they're above me." Before anyone could react, a blade flashed through the air.

Gilbert's vision narrowed. He ripped back and stared at the two jagged nubs. That's not right. Where were his fingers? A warm blanket of pain covered him. It started to grow. His knees gave out and he collapsed. It felt as if his hand had been forced into a fire that was only getting hotter. He tried to stand.

"See that? See that? Who's laughing now?"

"Damnit Gustav. This is the reason you're about to lose control."

"How? To who? They love me here. They respect me. They fear me!"

"Because you pay the guns. What happens when the guns grow tired of all this?"

The initial shock was fading. Blood flowed down Gilbert's arm.

"What? Quit complaining boy, you're staining the carpet. Here," Gustav took Gilbert's hand and drove his cigar into the flesh. "Man! He sounds like a pig."

Gilbert rammed his head into Gustav's skull. The Butcher stumbled back and tripped over a box.

"I'm not for sell!" The world blurred. "I'm not. I'm. I'm not. I'm not for sell."

Auriol began to laugh.

"I'll kill you." The Butcher struggled to sit up. Blood dripped from his broken nose. "I'll kill you!"

"You may want to run kid," said Auriol.

8 ... Hide and Seek

The Butcher's screams flooded the streets. Doors slammed. Lights went out. People hurried inside. Even the drunks hid. Gilbert ran to a house and pounded his fist against the wood.

"Open. Please. Ayúdame!" He tried another.

"Vete! No queremos problemas," said a woman. He kicked the door. Come on!

Wood exploded by his head. Another bullet whizzed past. Gilbert jumped over the railing and ran into the alleys.

Think. He had to get out of town before someone got hurt. The ranch? No. The old man wouldn't help. What if he took a horse?

He heard dogs barking.

No, a horse wouldn't do. He'd still be stuck on the island. Wait! Gilbert dug into his pocket and pulled out the boat key. If he could make it to the ship he might have a chance. He waited for the mob to pass and then made for the docks. The dull lamps cast just enough light to see names. *La Ballena. Última Esperanza. Cangrejos.* Where was it? *Mis Esperanzas. La Vieja Señora.*

"Hola."

Gilbert stopped walking and looked up.

A child, no more than ten and wearing a dirty orange and white striped shirt, stared at him from on top a stack of boxes.

"Hola," the boy said again. "Qué haces?"

Gilbert moved past the initial surprise and translated the question.

"Nothing," he answered. "What are you doing? You need to hide."

"I'm guarding these boats."

"You need to leave."

"No I don't. Hey. Are you that fighter, Caster? Papa says you're a bad person. He says you kill people."

"No, I—" Did people really think that? He could hear Gustav's men shouting. "Kid you really need to go."

"Why are they yelling? Are they happy? Are they playing a game? Oh! I want to play! I want to play!" The kid opened his mouth real wide. Gilbert dove and covered the tiny face with his hand.

"No! No. Don't yell. Please don't yell." He had an idea. "Yes. Yes. We're playing a game. We're playing hide and seek. You know that game, right? You know hide and seek?"

The child nodded. Gilbert removed his hand and said to hide and make no noise. Giggling, the child scurried off and hid under some tarps. Small feet poked out. It would have to do. Gilbert returned to the ships and found the *Sin Timón.*

What a sorry vessel. Empty bottles. Black and red mold. An inch of green water. He nearly slipped on a layer of slime.

"This way!"

Gilbert grabbed a sheet and threw it over himself just as the first man arrived. A thin slit allowed him to see their shoes.

"Span out. We heard voices this way." The wood creaked under their weight and the rattle of chains grew louder. Two muddied boots and a set of massive paws came his way. Gilbert held his breath and prayed. He was sure they could hear his heart.

A black tipped nose swept back and forth, coming closer and closer. It stopped and turned. Darkness enveloped as the dog's muzzle filled the slit. Hot, moist air blasted Gilbert's face.

The dog began to growl.

Gilbert imagined what came next. He reckoned he'd get bit at least once before he put the mutt down, and that was only if he somehow managed to avoid the men. Best to use his arm as a shield. After that he'd go for whoever the boots belonged to. Hopefully they had a gun. Take that, use the boxes as shelter, make his final stand on the docks. He should've never left home.

A shrill whistle sounded and the mouth was yanked away.

"See those feet?"

Feet? Feet!

The thunderclap of metal shattered the night.

"Looks a little young."

"Ah…stupid kid. Keep moving."

Gilbert remained still long after they left. His body refused to function. The kid had to be okay. They wouldn't shoot a child. Yeah. Yeah?

Breathe.

He rose, shaking, keeping his eyes focused on the water. He struggled to insert the key but finally managed and the boat's engine started with a pop and whiz. With that Gilbert Casanova set out into the night just as it started to rain.

Part 3
Layla London

November 8, 2021

9 ... Into the Storm

Not even Hell could be this terrible.

With each bolt of light and concussive blast the tiny ship shuddered, its final fate at the complete mercy of sea and storm. Violent winds and violent waves sent black liquid pouring inside. Bucket after bucket Gilbert fought to keep himself afloat. He was becoming numb. He had to. To think logically, to accept he was fighting a losing battle, would only bring about the end that much sooner. Fight. Fight! Just outlast the storm. After that... he'd worry about after that, after that.

"Come on!" he yelled. "That all you got? That the best you can do?"

The sky howled. Another wave crashed, knocking him off his feet. He could feel the ship struggling to hold. If the ocean didn't swallow man and ship it would certainly rip them to shreds.

He searched the rolling hills for safety. There had to be land. There had to be. Lightning streaked across the sky revealing the shadow of a mountain. He could make it. He could make it. Gilbert tied the bucket down and picked up a paddle.

Latching his foot around a metal bar so he was not slung free, Gilbert inched towards land. To the left. Now the right! Don't slap the water. Deep strokes. That's it!

Surge exploded in his face. Cloth stuck to skin. Salt burned his throat.

What a sight! Never had he seen a mountain so large, so dark, so dominating, so- so-

His soul began to shake.

Did it- did it move?

The wall of black towered over him like a boot over a spider. Man and ship lurched forward. Gilbert threw all his strength into the paddle. He began to rise. Wood snapped in his hands. Higher. He gripped the vessel's sides. Higher. Jagged plastic ate into flesh. Higher and higher. With every flash the peak grew nearer.

For a split-second Gilbert could see everything. In all directions was wild, untamable sea. Any hope vanished. The ship stopped vibrating. Winds calmed. All was silent. Then just as suddenly he found himself plummeting towards the abyss.

The nose smacked the surface, crunching plastic and metal. Water flooded. Gilbert filled his lungs with air and was pulled under.

10 ... The Captain

"He's coming 'round. Give 'em space."

Gilbert vomited water and tried to breathe. Everything hurt. He continued to groan and assess his senses. What happened? Where was he? The last thing he remembered was going up a wave then falling.

"Come on, man," said a voice, "I just cleaned that."

His eyes came into focus. Three men in identical blue sweaters and orange overalls huddled around him. Gilbert tried to move but found himself wrapped in blankets.

"Easy there. Grab 'em before he hurts himself."

Strange hands reached out.

"Tell the captain he's up. It's Gilbert, right?"

How did they know his name? The Butcher. No! He wasn't going back.

Gilbert reared his legs and kicked the closet man, sending the stranger crashing into a wall. He bit the other.

"Puto!" A fist connected with Gilbert's jaw.

"Enough." A fourth man entered. He carried himself with a swagger that spoke both confidence and experience, with a touch for theatrics but little ego. "That's enough. Tella, bandage your arm. Cecil, Devin." The men left. The captain, Gilbert assumed, leaned against a table. "You're a hard man to find, Señor Casanova. Very hard. I hear Gustav put a pretty price on your head. Not enough to retire, of course, but maybe a decent vacation or fancy watch or whatever you might like." He looked at Gilbert and smiled. "How does thirty-thousand sols sound?"

Gilbert leaned back. "They tried to sell me for eighty. If I were you, I wouldn't bother. Not worth the paperwork."

"Well, lucky for us no paperwork is involved in these sorts of transactions. But it would be a hassle. I'd have to take you there, which costs gas. Listen to Gustav gloat or try to impart wisdom or whatever he feels, blah blah blah. He'd probably make me stay to watch you die, which is just tiresome. But – and this is the catch – the fish just aren't biting this year. See, I've got pockets to fill, mouths to feed. I'm sure you understand." He clapped his hands. "Where are my manners? Pablo Escuella, captain of the

Roach. You already met my father. Cranky old bastard. How's the ranch looking?"

Gilbert's nostrils flared. The old man. "Mad I took his boat?"

"He wants to kill you just as bad as Gustav. Maybe worse."

The single bulb swayed with the waves. Outside, the hum of the ocean mixed with music. Leaving America was the worst decision he ever made. Right now he'd probably be fast asleep in his nice bed, food in the fridge, clean clothes in his closet. Instead, he was about to be delivered back to hell.

The captain broke into laughter. "I apologize. Just having a little fun, señor. No, he is not mad. Quite the opposite. My father buys cheap boats and helps get some of you lot out. Trackers in the life jackets, though you'd be surprised how many don't wear them. My job is to scoop you up."

Gilbert was cautious. It seemed too good, and he'd come to distrust those situations. "If you're not taking me back, where are we going?"

"Dorado."

His breath caught. Dorado? After all this time?

The captain continued. "It'll be a week or so. Picked a hell of a time to skip town. Between us, my father didn't think you'd make it. Once you're rested I'll fill you in on what's next. Get you situated. Until then sleep, heal, eat. If you need anything I'll be somewhere above." Pablo left.

Gilbert laid down and let his muscles relax for the first time in weeks. He felt lighter. A large smile stretched from ear to ear. Dorado. Dorado! Forget the pain! Forget the scars! None of that mattered now. He was going to Dorado. To Layla London. To Womack's treasure. Months of struggle, and now he was on the doorstep.

Darkness closed in and he drifted off to sleep.

11 ... Nightmares and Witches

"You failed us, Gilbert Casanova. You left us to die."

The air was warm and dry. Almost stale, in a way. As if something lurked nearby, watching, waiting. Gilbert looked around. Endless fields of wheat stretched out under clear blue skies. Again, the voice whispered.

"You left us to rot. To decay."

"Hello? Think you have the wrong person." He began walking South. "Where am I?"

Silence.

"Anyone ther—," The air caught in his throat.

"You betrayed us. Forgot us. Cast us aside."

He dropped to the ground, clawing, rolling. "I- I- I didn't."

More voices joined. Hands sprouted from the earth.

"Failure. Abandoner. Monster. Impudent. Languisher. You sacrificed us."

"N- No." His sight flickered. Slowly he was pulled under the earth.

"You will pay. We have not forgot."

"No!" Gilbert fell onto the floor. The world rocked back and forth and took shape. The boat. He was still on Pablo's ship. It was a dream. It was just a dream. He took long breaths until his heart settled.

He grabbed a box for support and lifted himself up, pushing the nightmare from his mind. There were more important things to worry about.

The door swung open.

"Ah good, you're up," said the captain. He tossed Gilbert a bag. "Figured you might want some clean clothes. Got breakfast topside whenever you're hungry."

Gilbert pulled out a red-gray poncho with crude condors down the front. The soft hair was cool against his skin. Carefully, he made his way up the stairs. He crashed into a wall. Land. He wanted – no – needed land. How could anyone stay upright on these things?

The smell of sea and fish and work was a welcome change. No manure. No cheap alcohol. No La Guera. Freedom.

"See! I told you he wasn't a vampire. Pay up," yelled one of the men.

The other, Tella, dug a bandaged arm into his pocket and pulled out a clump of colorful notes. "Can't be too careful these days. Already have a witch on the loose."

"Mate, if he was a vampire, you'd be a vampire. You don't want him to be a vampire."

"All I'm saying is you can't be too careful. Just last week I saw a sea monster a few miles out. Beautiful creature. Scales like a rainbow. Teeth like swords. Neck as thick as trees."

"Mate, the day you see a sea monster is the day a beautiful woman falls for me."

"What are you trying to say?"

"That you're crazy."

Gilbert took a seat. "Sorry to disappoint but I'm actually a werewolf." Their laughs reassured him.

"You joke, but let me tell you boy, these things aren't laughing matters. Witches, vampires, sea monsters – even your 'werewolf' – they're all true."

"Oh, back off the kid. He doesn't know. Gilbert, help yourself to some fish and bread. Nice to see you finally get a little daylight."

Gilbert filled a plate and ate. It was decent, but the fish needed flavoring. "What don't I know?"

Tella lowered his voice. "The bruja is real. She haunts the island."

Gilbert struggled to contain his amusement. Witches? How young did they think he was? "Sure, and I have a fairy godmother."

No one laughed. No one smiled. They all stared at the ground.

"I never seen her, but I hear stories. They say water turn to blood when she touch it. That she arrive after eating all the babies on Isla Cordo."

"Aye, heard that. Diego said when she shoot Guido's pigs, she said it didn't die right. Wanted to keep going until one did."

"Diego saw it? Diego!"

A gruff looking man joined the group.

"Si, I seen it. The witch- The witch uses this spell ta trick us. Takes the form of a young woman ta seduce weak minds. I was under it for a while cause I was so close, you see. But one night I was out walking and heard this scream coming from the volcano. Screams that froze me where I stood. I realized that must be its lair. I get close and in the shadows I see this creature, this- this- It had the body of a dog and the head of a rabbit. Hair made of fire. Wings. Short little fat wings. Like- Like- What's the bird that can't fly? Black and white."

"Penguin?"

"That one! Yes. Wings like a penguin. This thing, it was dancing real weird, shouting something in a language I didn't know. The place was glowing. I realized it was doing its spells and I just seen its true form."

"How are you alive?" Tella asked.

"I don't know. I must've been too far or the Lord was on my side or just got lucky."

The men nodded.

"I went to grab my gun but when I got back, it was gone. Poof! Like nothing ever happened."

"Gilbert," The captain strutted over and the group fell silent. "Hope I'm not interrupting. Walk with me."

12 ... Dorado

In the distance was the outline of a great black mountain.

"Beauty, isn't she?" said the captain. "Should reach town in an hour or so. I talked to miss London yesterday and she wants to see about you maybe working with her. She has meetings for most of the morning and into the afternoon, so we'll grab lunch before I send you on up."

Gilbert's stomach twisted and limbs tingled. Layla London. The Layla London. He was actually going to meet her. This was it. This was his chance. Think. What books did she write? What awards has she won?

Fleets of fishing boats bobbed while bronzed sailors unloaded the morning's catch. Peruvian vendors cheerfully shouted from stone streets to the women bathing on pastel roofs that would laugh and call out in response. Tight brick alleys were filled with every food and smell imaginable — colorful fruits, dripping meats, pungent spices, sizzling fish. In the large, manicured center square waved the red-white-red flag of Peru and the island's own gold-black-blue standard. Church bells sang out on the hour with such authority and awe that even the old men stopped to listen. Children chased each other up and down carved stairs. Wives shouted at their husbands. Dogs roamed the streets. Gilbert had never seen a place so alive.

Now Pablo wobbled while Gilbert walked straight. He never cared for water. Couldn't even swim that well. All the terrors and unknowns and Tella's 'sea monsters' lurking beneath the surface. And not just the big things. Growing up, his grandmother would tell a story of a promising young athlete that went swimming in a lake and caught some brain eating amoeba. Gilbert shivered at the thought. Horrible way to go out.

They stopped in front of a red door marked ALVEREZ BAR and went inside.

It was cheerful enough. White spotted walls, clean wood floors – if overly waxed or whatever the term was – pictures of family and friends. A group of hunched men played dominos in a corner, heavy smoke flowing up from their fingers and out an open window. Against the front wall was a simple wooden bar guarded by a short fat woman, and the smell of spices and meat escaped from the kitchen.

The captain raised his arms and shouted. "Lucia! How lovely you look."

The bartender pursed her lips. "Go to hell Pablo."

"Ah, pay no attention to her señor. She loves me. Come, let's grab a table. Two ceviche, por favor! Beer? No? Water!"

One of the patrons yelled across the room. "Bring another bruja, Escuella? Keep picking up strays and you gonna get yourself killed."

Pablo waved them off.

At first Gilbert assumed the witch talk was a bunch of nonsense, just the sailors trying to scare him. But now…

"What do you think about this 'witch'?"

"Guess there's not much else to talk about. I don't believe all the stories, and neither should you. But there's something off about her."

"So she's real? Is she a doctor?"

"Doctor? No, she's…no."

"Is she a killer or something?"

"No. Well…she's Layla's apprentice. I'm sure you'll cross paths at some point."

"Is she a criminal? What makes her so bad?"

"I don't know. None of us really do."

"There has to be something. Is she just ugly?"

"To be quite honest only a handful have seen her, and I think most wish it to remain so. Aye, she's disfigured, muscled, but I've met plenty of worse looking folks that I've taken no issue with. So again, I don't know. She has eyes that either shine like emeralds or snarl like venom depending on the light, and the few times we've met she's been covered in dirt and blood. Yet most on this island work the earth, so it's not her appearance that gets me, though I'm sure it plays a part. Just thinking about her makes my skin crawl and spine shake. Even her name leaves a bitter taste in my mouth. Angela. An-gee-la. Like an angel that couldn't cut it. I've never met a soul I so dislike, but I couldn't tell you why. I wish I could, truthfully. It's almost like a shadow or stench that follows her around. People become sick. Children scream and run. Animals die. Things go wrong. Maybe that's it. Maybe that's what she is. A disease. A curse. One thing's for certain, though, she isn't who she claims to be."

The captain sunk back into his seat and swallowed his drink. "But let's not dwell on such things. The witch hasn't been seen in weeks. Perhaps we're rid of her." He called for another beer. "What got you interested in Miss London? I've seen a number of people come thinking they have what it takes to continue her legacy. None have managed."

"Sophomore year of high school I had a teacher, Mister Lambert — awesome guy — and he required we read *Adventures in*

India. Hooked immediately. Started reading anything of her's I could. Made me want to be an adventurer." Just talking about it made the dream seem possible. "What about this apprentice? Wouldn't she be next in line?"

Pablo's face twisted. "There are many moving parts, señor. From what I hear, if it's true, well...no. Forget it. My father spoke highly of you, which is a rare thing. You seem decent enough."

Gilbert shifted his thoughts to his meeting with Layla. "Any words of wisdom before I see her?"

"Honesty. London can sniff out a liar like a shark. If she smells blood, she'll feast."

13 ... High Expectations

Gilbert stopped walking.

Don't throw up. Don't throw up. Don't…oh…don't throw up. Lunch was a terrible idea. Breathe. Maybe it would pass.

No.

He fell to his knees and vomited. Minutes later he sat back wiping sweat and rain and food from his face.

"You're good." He steadied himself. His eyes remained fixed on the white speck at the base of the volcano. "You'll be fine. Tell a few jokes. Be excited. Be honest. You got this."

Twenty minutes later he reached the building. Beneath a lone table a gray-haired dog raised its head and barked. Gilbert knelt and scratched behind its ear.

"Hey there," he checked the collar, "Charlie? Charles? Funny name for a dog."

Charles licked his wrist. Gilbert gave the dog a final pat and went inside.

Row upon row of exotic trophies lined the walls. Sailing Pole to Pole. Soloing Everest without oxygen. Ritualistic combat in Africa. Rescuing survivors from a submarine. Discovering El Dorado.

Sitting polished behind the counter were three Nobel prizes - literature, physics, medicine. Above the split staircase hung the heads of lions and bears and various skins from Earth's deadliest predators. Elegant tapestries, royal gifts, exquisite works of art — all tossed wherever they could find space. Every relic, every picture, every handmade table and chair pointed back to one woman. One adventurer. The legendary Layla London.

All this. All this could be him. He saw himself scrounging through mosquito infested jungles. Harpooning whales with native Alaskans. Wrestling poachers and saving trapped elephants. He'd dine with kings, smile on red carpets, tell jokes and stories on all the talk shows. Faces would melt in awe and wonder at the terrifying and deadly life he lived. With a smirk, he'd reassure the masses that not once was he worried and everything always went according to plan. He'd write bestselling works, cure diseases, build modern marvels. He'd find lost cities. Uncover forgotten fortunes. Live an amazing, unmatched, glorious story. He was Gilbert Casanova! The smile faded. He was Gilbert Casanova. What did Gilbert Casanova know about anything?

He looked at the pictures and the trophies and the awards. All of this was above him. Way, way above him. He had no business being there. This was a waste of time. Leave. Find a way back to the States. Maybe his old job would take him back.

He turned to the door and froze.

14 ... Layla London

"You made it!" said Layla.

Her welcoming smile was betrayed by cautious yellow eyes that looked down on him. Blood, recently dried, covered dark overalls and the sleeves of the tired sweater hung loosely over her frame. White hair puffed out from under a bright orange beanie, and her wrinkled skin was deeply tanned. "I am so sorry I'm running late. Had meetings and ran into people and helped birth a cow. Sit! Sit! Hope you weren't waiting too long." She dashed behind the counter and cleaned herself. "I have some fresh bananas if you're hungry. Anything to drink?" She returned with a bowl of fruit. "So. How are you? Did you ride or walk?"

Gilbert's muscles tightened and turned to jelly. Speak. Say something. "I- I walked, Miss London."

"Should've guessed. From what I hear you had quite a time getting to the island. Oh, and before we get going I'll go ahead and put a stop to any 'Miss London' malarky. It's Layla. Anything more makes me feel old. Now, I understand you came from La Guerra. How'd you end up there?"

"Stumbled onto it."

"Stumbled onto it? How does an American – I'm guessing American – stumble onto an island off the coast of Peru? And La Guerra no less?"

Gilbert recalled Pablo's advice. "Spent the past couple of months looking for you. Started out in Columbia, then Brazil. Argentina. Back to Brazil. Chile. Peru. Met a guy in Cusco who said you were on an island out here. First went to Isla Uno, Del Rio, then La Guerra. Ran into the Butc-. A man who said he could get me here, and, well, things didn't go quite as planned."

"I know of Gustav. No need to dance around it. If you don't mind me asking, who was he going to sell you to?"

"How'd you kn- "

"Pablo told me. Don't feel like you have to answer. Just curious."

"Man named Auriol Silver, I think."

She closed her eyes. "Oh, Gabrielle…"

"If you know, why haven't you told the world about him?"

She opened her eyes and smiled. "Afraid it's not that easy. Gustav and the people he works with have their hands in a lotta different pockets. Some've tried but things never really end well. Pablo, myself, others, we do what we can. I'm just glad you're okay and here. But let's keep things moving. Where you from?"

Her answer didn't sit well but he held his tongue. "Knoxville, Tennessee. Chattanooga originally."

"Get out. I'm from Asheville. Did you ever hike the Smokey's?"

"All the time. Used to do Mount Le Conte for fun."

"Which way did you go?"

"Alum Cave."

"Fun stuff. Beautiful place. And what brought you down here?"

"To find you and—"

"No no. What drove you to leave home?"

He shifted in his seat. "Dad died. Figured no time like the present to see the world."

"Sorry to hear that. How was the funeral?"

"It was sad," he lied. "How'd you end up here?"

"Oh, this and that. Meet someone who knows somebody. One thing leads to another." She took a sip of her drink. "You said you were looking for me. Why?"

A million different reasons danced in his head. "I- You- I- One second." Should he mention the treasure? No. Not yet. "How do I be like you? Ever since I first read your books I thought that's someone I wanna be. All the stories. All the pictures. All the movies. Yeah, the fame seems cool and all, but it's more than that. It's that desire for life. It's that keep goingness. You never settle. How? Even now you just radiate this energy. I want that. I want that life where I'm always doing. Always giving. Always meeting different people and pushing myself and growing. I don't wanna get to your age and be like man, I wish I'd done x, y, and z but didn't."

Layla leaned in her chair and closed her eyes. Without looking at him she finally spoke. "What do you mean 'your age'? Sorry, old person joke. One thing immediately comes to mind. You don't need me for that. When I started I had no idea what I was doing. I just went. And screwed up a ton. I don't have some se- cret formula because there isn't one. You explore. You meet peo- ple. You smile and try to be kind. There's a bit more to it than that, but that's the gist. Keep your head on a swivel. Trust your gut. Pack extra socks—"

"And filter water. I've read your book." He hadn't come this far to fail now.

"Many have." There was pity in her voice. She looked at her wrist. "Do you have a place to stay tonight?"

Gilbert's mind went blank. The thought never occurred to him.

"Tell you what. I've got a spare bed. Nothing special but it'll do. Stay the night and I'll think about what you said. Deal? Let me show you the room."

Layla led him outside and around the building and into a rough two-storied garage. There was a slight buzz when the power flickered on. A single window and plastic roofing filtered sunlight throughout the wide living area. Kitchen, bathroom, lounge, beds were all squeezed into one. Against the far side was a dusty desk and a single chair. The walls were cracked and bare save for a singular picture of a camel above one bed.

"Here we are. Don't mess with anything on the other side of the room, that's someone else's. I'm helping hunt guineas in the morning, so Charles and I are staying in town which means you're on your own. There's a phone and address book in my office, and I keep food below the bar if you get hungry. Oh, one last little tiny thing, and I'm embarrassed I even have to say it, but don't steal anything. I'll leave you to it."

He sat down on the hard mattress and stared at the discolored ceiling. Tiny black bugs fell like droplets. For ten minutes he flicked them away but eventually gave up, his mind analyzing the whole conversation. Was he convincing? Did he say something wrong? She would've said yes by now. She was going to toss him, wasn't she? He fell back and rubbed his cheeks. "You're good. I'm sure she'll say yes." Yes to what? Helping him? If she let him stay, how was he supposed to bring up Womack casually? And what if she didn't? He might not get another chance to learn anything.

Gilbert rolled over. Just stay in the room. Don't snoop.

The hours ticked away.

What the hell. No one would know.

15 ... The Art of Thievery

Moonlight bounced off priceless decorations, giving the place the feel of some backstage theatre or forgotten warehouse. Any second Gilbert expected something to pop out from behind a table or one of the mounted heads to come to life. This was insane. Was he really about to steal from his hero?

He entered the dark-wooded, book lined study. The embers of a dying fire glowed orange in the stone alcove. Making his way to the large desk, he shined his light over the open books and scattered papers.

Lists. Exports. Reminders. Nothing useful.

He studied the shelves. Several titles he recognized as ones he had back home. He took down a copy of *Treasure Island* and flipped through the pages. He'd read it once but didn't care for the ending. Too drawn out and too happy. He placed it back in its spot and grabbed *The Odyssey*. The wall groaned and opened.

His heart skipped a beat.

Inside were neatly stacked boxes. Gilbert brought his light close to the faint writing. *Peru - April, 1983. Nepal - December, 1989. Madagascar - July, 2014.* He pulled one labelled *Antarctica - December, 2004.*

Broken gear. Old pictures. A plastic cup. Brown journal.

December 20, 2004 - Day 32.

It's cold. David is sick. Asked us to leave him behind for the polar bears. Told him I respect the animals too much. Spirits are good. Landscape is still barren in a beautiful way. Never gets old.

He went for another.

Asheville - 1980 thru 1982. He picked up a faded picture. A young woman smiled on top of a mountain. As he slid the contents back the box refused to fit. He pushed harder. A small door popped open and a black journal fell out. How many secrets did this woman have?

'BLACK LILY' was written across the front. He opened to the first page.

I shall attempt to record all I can regarding the whereabouts of the Pirate Womack's Treasure.

This was it!

He flipped through. Something about keys. North Carolina. Alaska. France. It was all here.

Gilbert stuffed the book into his pocket and made sure nothing looked out of place.

A light came on. "Find what you were looking for?"

He nearly collapsed. "This bathroom doesn't have a toilet."

"Maybe because it's not a bathroom." Layla shook her head. "I'll give you points for originality but you really need to work on your lies. Come on, let's see it."

He could feel heat rush to his face and desperation to his stomach. Gilbert reached into his jacket and handed her the book.

"Most go for the jewels. Every now and then it's one of the Nobels. Caught a group sneaking out with a Persian rug once, that was funny. But no one's ever gone for a journal." She looked at him. "So why you? If I offered you every treasure in this building or this journal, which would you choose?"

"Journal." He took a deep breath. "Miss London. Sorry. Layla. I wasn't completely honest earlier."

"Hmph."

"I did — do — really wanna find you. And I do want your help and your guidance. But I really, really wanna find this treasure."

"Why? Money?"

"No."

"Fame."

"No."

"Then why? Why go through all the trouble."

"I don't know. Really, I don't. It's just this feeling, that I have to find it. Or die trying. It's crazy, I know."

Layla's eyes twinkled and a great big smile crossed her face. "I have two regrets in life. One, never having kids, and two, never finding this. Bit late for the former, but the latter? Well, I've got a little left in the tank. What do you say, up for an adventure?"

16 ... The Witch of Dorado

"You failed us, Gilbert. You left us to die."

Gilbert woke in a cold sweat. The dreams were becoming frequent. Food, rest, and better company would surely fix it. He checked the time. Six-fifteen.

He cranked the shower to its highest setting and massaged the muscles of his face until it was free of sleep. After drying and changing he made his way to the bar and prepared a large breakfast of cold oatmeal, two orange bananas, and half a plate of leftover salmon. He brought the meal back to his room and ate while pouring over the journal.

The more he dug, the less human Womack became. He was brutal. The few he respected were given a quick death. Others he would hack apart bit by bit using a wire to make their eyes pop and then feed whatever was left to fourteen dogs. For three years he sailed around the world terrorizing villages and exploring remote lands. References ranged from Madagascar all the way to the tribes of North Alaska. And then in 1627 he vanished. A few mentions of the name *Charles*. A handful of lovers. A ship's name. No descriptions or family. As for the treasure, all he had to go by was a note about keys and a riddle. He recalled his conversation with Layla.

"The keys," she said, "they're not exactly keys in the modern sense. Think more like a tool, each about, I don't know, ten, eleven inches in length. Six across," she showed the dimensions with her hands. "Two triangles. Each has a system of mirrors inside that reflect light. I don't know what they show — a location, a password — but they're needed to access the treasure room."

"And you know this how?"

"About ten years back I found L'or des Fous, and, well," she lifted her shirt to reveal a white scar running across her stomach. "You can't get in without the keys."

Gilbert winced at the sight, but also felt a jolt of excitement.

"Any idea what they look like?"

Layla went to the shelves and pulled down a thick leather book. She flipped through the thin pages and stopped on an aged drawing. The black piece looked to be a treasure itself. Golden flowers were carved along the sides, and sapphires lined the bottom.

A series of barks from outside snapped him back to attention.

"Oh calm down ya ugly mutt. No. Abajo. Abajo! Ya do this every damn time Chuck. How'd ya like it if I did the jumping, huh?"

He hid the journal under his pillow.

The door flew open. "Look! The cripple's up."

A young woman with orange hair and bright green eyes stood in the entrance. Her left-hand scooped peanut butter into her mouth from of a jar lodged under her shoulder while the thumb of her right-hand raced between the webbing of the middle and ring fingers. Dirty blue cloth sagged out from a heavy jacket and overlapped greasy cargo pants that folded irregularly onto wrinkled boots. A black revolver was holstered on her hip.

"Holy snot shells and a tractor trailer, talk about a hike, am I right? Oh, don't give me that look. Everyone gives me that look. My mama gave me that look. Hell, even Layla gives me that look. Well, I've never seen her give it ta me, but I know she does. I bet as soon as I walk away she does. Hey, are ya just gonna sit there and stare? Smile? Frown? Blink? Can ya blink? Who are ya? I'm Angela. Hold on. Hola? Olá? Bonjour? Nĭ hǎo? Any of those? I'm running out of languages. I know ya can talk. Ya talk in ya sleep. Ya a little fat, ya know? Not that that's a problem. Well…back up. I know a lotta fat people. Most people in town are fat, but I don't know their names. Rather not. Feeling's mutual, ta be honest. Come ta think of it, ya not fat. Ya not ripped, but ya alright, ya know?" She shoveled a fistful of peanut butter into her mouth. "I don't eat meat anymore. Protein. Am I being weird?"

What was happening? "A little."

Her face turned red. "Damnit. Let's start over. Shalom. My name is Angela J. Bronte. I don't know ya, but ya in my room." She wiped her hand on her jacket and stuck it out with a big smile.

Angela. Angela! The eyes!

She grabbed his arm, put his hand in hers, and shook.

"One sec." She stepped outside. Before the door finished swinging a long, loud squeak sounded. "It's the dairy or the spices or maybe both, I don't know, ya know. Doesn't sit well but it's so good. I was grabbing a cup and these two local chicks kept looking at me funny. They were bolth like 'it's her it's her' and I was like 'it's me it's me'. Ya shoulda seen the dresses they had on." She stuck out her tongue. "Shoot me if I ever dress like that off job, will ya?" Her stare narrowed. "Kentucky?"

Kentucky?

"Ya accent. Ya from Kentucky?"

"Oh. Tennessee. New Jersey?"

"York. Hell's Kitchen."

"Ah. City girl."

"Ehh. Not exactly. Grew up on an island not far from here. What gave it away?"

"Bolth. It's pronounced 'both'. No 'L'."

"Well, 'bolth' ways get the point across. Ya don't see me arguing about how 'ain't y'all just the sweetest peach, I do declare' or whatever y'all cousin lovers do. Hey, check this out." She tossed him a silver talisman with a ruby center. "Old Chinese shipwreck. Sharks everywhere. The locals were pretty narrowed minded about the whole thing." She removed her jacket and made a face. "Gosh that stinks. Yeah, the past few weeks I've been hunting that bad boy down. No big deal, ya know. Just living on the bare minimum. Danger at every turn." She continued to change. Before Gilbert averted his eyes he noticed a number of scars on her back. "I keep telling Layla she should meet me when I arrive. I hate walking through town." She whistled. "Good looking ceiling, huh?"

"Admiring the cracks and stuff."

"Sure ya are."

Say something. Anything.

"Well I do declare. It would appear I have stumped mister—Ya know, I don't think I ever got ya name?"

"Gilbert. Gilbert Casanova."

"Gilbert Casa— I'm just gonna call ya Cas. Well, mister Cas. Nah, I don't like that. Nova? No. Gil. Oh! Gilby. That's a keeper." She cleaned her glasses with her shirt. "Gilby, around these parts looking don't get ya in trouble. Touching might."

Gilbert swallowed the lump in his throat. "You work for Layla?"

She rolled her eyes. "Sí. I'm what the peo— Do ya like Christmas music? I love the stuff." She took out her phone and turned up the volume. He could hardly hear himself think. "I'm what the people call a purveyor of rare items. And some not so rare. But yeah, I work for the amazing, great, holier-than-thou Layla London. Kinda do the less glamorous jobs, ya know. Things she doesn't want the world ta see."

Things she doesn't want the world to see? "Sounds like a thief."

Grunting, Angela hopped on the other bed. The frame shook while she tried to make herself comfortable. "Thief? Thief? Gilby, ya wound me. Such a harsh word, thief. I personally prefer morally gray opportunist. If no one ever knew it existed, is it really stealing? If ya found a hundred dollars on the street, would ya keep it? No. Ya'd do the Christian thing and turn it in'ta wine. I just know where ta look and how ta extract. I don't break in'ta peoples' homes and all that. Anymore, at least. And besides, the all great benefactor thought it was better for me."

84

"Better than what?"

"Nothing!" As she flipped around a curtain of orange unfolded and piled on the floor. Her body arched to match that of an unfinished jigsaw puzzle.

"Sorry. I've heard so much about a witch and, well, you're not what I expected."

The smile vanished and she wiggled her fingers at him. "What, not enough warts? Too young? Trying ta figure out where I store the bones of my victims? Holy whores, what else they saying about me now?" She started to pick at her nails. "Ya meet my expectations, ya know? A straight prick. Enough about me. What brings ya ta this fine establishment? It's not sex, partying, or people, and ya don't strike me as the usual tourist. Work clothes. I've seen those before. Hell, I've worn those. So ya working with Layla. But the wide eyes? Obvious inexperience?" She squinted. "What's ya background?"

"Engineer."

"No. Phone background?"

Gilbert raised the screen. "Was backpacking though Alaska and my buddy wanted to climb that mountain."

"Backpack often?"

"Believe it or not it was my first time. See I was trying to impress this girl—"

"Yes or no. So adventurous but stupid, yet ya don't scream thrill seeker. And the way ya listen so closely, ya seem ta actually care about getting ta know me." Her eyes shot to his pillow then back to him. "So ya my new partner? How wonderful."

"Think you may be confused."

"So I'm told. Ya know, I'm excited. I think we'll get along just fine." She rolled over. "So where we going? Africa? Asia? The ol' Outback? Lays told me she gave ya a mission. Should be in a journal or something."

"She never mentioned a partner."

Angela groaned. "She does this all the time and I end up look-ing weird. Look, my job is ta help train ya, keep ya from dying, stuff like that. If I think ya do a decent job, I check a box and ya might get ta work with Layla. And I hate ta be that person, but clock's-a-ticking. We shoulda' been on the road hours ago."

He wasn't convinced. "If Layla wanted us to work together, shouldn't you already know where we're going?"

"Ya catch on fast! Part of training, amigo. Ya never know what ta expect. Have ta think on ya feet. Take charge. So, let's see it."

Gilbert took out the journal and tossed it across the room. An-gela's face darkened with each page.

"Maybe…," she whispered.

The witch? The witch? As far as introductions went it was far from his best. Wasn't his worst, though. That honor belonged to a first date where he thought it'd be funny to wear a clown nose. What an idiot. The girl was perfect — funny, smart, cute, driven — the whole package. And he went and ruined it with a clown nose. It'd been months since the disaster and still he wanted to strangle himself. Focus. Maybe he could salvage this.

"Hey, I want to apologize for the witch comment. I was surprised and it was poor form on my part. Care to start over?"

"Huh?" Her eyes raced around the room before stopping on him. "No. Yeah. All good."

"I think we should start in North Carolina. There's a riddle—"

"*Beneath the roots where my lily once grew, there my key awaits you.* There's an old group called the Order of the Lilies in Charleston. Some meet every year at this big Christmas ball, ya know. Might be connected. And it just so happens that I took care of the host's wife and kids a few years back."

"It's November."

"Ya got a better plan?"

Gilbert tried to contain his excitement. Secret orders. Balls. Riddles!

Part 4
North Carolina

November 24, 2021

17 ... Home Cooking

The distant blue shadows of the smokey mountains dominated the rearview mirror. A few hours in that direction would get Gilbert to Knoxville. To friends, to work, to life, to home. He wiped the layers of humidity from his face and checked what exit they needed to get off.

"Ya Americans are weird, ya know?" Angela stared at the passing billboards with disgust. "I mean, get the body ya want... fast. Just go ta a gym! Or that one, two burgers for the price of one. Not ta mention I can hardly breathe. All these cars..." She went back to picking her nails.

"Two burgers doesn't sound bad. We haven't ate since the island."

"Sure we did. And we only have three hours left. This exit."

"I know." He pulled off. "And a bag of cookies doesn't count."

Gilbert tried to ignore his growling stomach, but the passing restaurants only made it worse. Three hours? Sure, she could sleep while he drove but God forbid he takes five minutes to get some food. Stop. Be positive. It felt refreshing to drive on smooth asphalt after months of dirt paths.

His eyes widened. "No way."

"What?"

"They have a Champions here."

"A what?"

"Champions. It's fried chicken. There's one in Knoxville that we hit up all the time in college."

"No."

Gilbert pulled into the parking lot.

"Turn this car around."

He parked the car, cracked a window, and shut off the engine.

"I will not eat that stuff. And we're wasting time."

He shut the door and headed inside.

The smells of grease and chicken and pork and spices greeted him. Hundreds of signed dollar bills were nailed to wooden beams, and pictures of random celebrities filled the walls. Every beer imaginable sat in rows behind the counter. Empty peanut shells littered the floors.

"Be right with ya honey," yelled a gray haired lady.

"No rush," he called back.

She returned wiping her hands on her apron. "Alright, how are we today? Just one?"

"Two. She's still in the car."

The lady grabbed two menus and motioned for him to follow. "Let me tell you now, if my boys left their ladies in the car, oh lord, there'd be hell to pay. Is this good?"

Gilbert sat at the checkerboard table. "This is perfect, thank you. Can we go ahead and get two waters?"

"Sure thing. Do you need a minute or do you know what you want?"

He glanced at the menu. Nothing had changed. "Two four-piece baskets, please. Can we get extra fries instead of coleslaw? Thanks."

The lady walked away.

Gilbert sunk back in his chair and smiled. College football played on a nearby tv. Alabama was up against LSU.

The door chimed.

"He's to the left honey."

Angela walked in and dropped into the seat across from him. A thin line of blood was starting to pool on her thumb. "How'd she know I was with ya?"

Gilbert shrugged. "I don't know. They just do." He went back to watching the game. He noticed Angela couldn't sit still, constantly turning to look at the door. "Wanna switch chairs?"

"What? No. How long is this gonna be?"

"I don't know? Half an hour? You good? You seem a little off."

Since leaving the island she had grown aggressive.

"I'm fine," she hissed.

"It's just food. We got plenty of time."

The lady returned with two baskets of golden chicken and fries. Gilbert grabbed the top piece and bit in. Juices burned his mouth and set his throat on fire. He took another bite. He couldn't recall a better tasting meal.

Angela pushed her basket away.

"Crap." Gilbert looked for a napkin and, not seeing one, wiped grease on his pants. He noted the crumbs around his basket. He really was a messy eater. "Oh, you hate to see it."

"See what?" Angela went back to looking around. "What is it."

Gilbert pointed at the tv. "Arsenal. Lost to Tottenham this morning."

94

"What?"

"Arsenal. The socc- football team. English. Friend of mine is a big fan."

Angela rolled her eyes and slumped. She hadn't even tasted her food. Gilbert could hear the rapid taps of her foot from under the table.

"Watch any sports?"

"Why?"

"I don't know. Can be fun. Something to talk about."

"Gilbert, I don't have time for stuff like that. It's all a waste."

"Well, what do you enjoy?"

"Not this."

The feeling was becoming mutual.

Her head whipped around as the door chimed again. A loud, overweight family waddled through.

"How ya doin' Pearl? Ya'll doin' alright today? Don't seem too busy."

"Oh we're doing fine Bruce. Lucy, that dress looks great on you. Y'all sit wherever."

They pulled two tables together. "Zane here just got second chair for his school's band. Best trombone player in the state!"

Angela leaned in. "How can someone live like that? I mean, that's embarrassing."

"Bit harsh, don't you think? Yeah, might not be the healthiest, but they seem happy. Can't go around judging people at first glance. Hell, when we first met you looked like crap."

"I'd just walked five miles and found some stranger in my room. Shamu over there is out of breath from just standing up." The cut on her thumb had grown larger. "And second? If that were my child, we'd be back home practicing 'till his little fat fingers bled. Can we please go? We're gonna be late."

Gilbert finished his meal and paid the check for both him and the other family, much to Angela's dislike.

The next three hours were spent in silence punctuated only by the phone giving directions. Suburbs gave way to rolling fields and farms. Houses went from identical to sparse to large multi-storied mansions.

"It'll be the next right," said Angela.

Tall green hedges hid what lay inside. Gilbert turned down a gravel road and continued straight until he reached an iron fence. He hit the speaker. "Gilbert Casanova and Angela Bronte here to see the Honorable Reginald R. R. Robertson." The name was the most pretentious thing he'd ever spoken. The gates opened.

A canopy of willow trees lined either side of the black road leading to the two-level plantation house. Most of the original structure and columns looked to be present, but large additions had been added on either side. Empty fields sprawled out for miles.

Gilbert stopped in front of the white stairs. A well-dressed man made his way down and opened Angela's door. "Evening madame. My name is Bernard Cutlasbee. The Honor is currently overseeing personal matters and will call on you at his earliest convenience."

Gilbert got himself out and grabbed the bags.

"Please sir, allow me."

"It's all good Bernard. This ain't really my style, so I apologize if I say or do something wrong."

"Ah! Not the accent I was expecting. Are you from around here?"

"Knoxville. Grew up in Chattanooga."

"I met my wife in Chattanooga. Fine town. This way please." He led them away from the main building. "You must excuse the walk. With tonight's party the Honor already agreed to let a number of guests stay. Your rooms are at the far end. I'm sure they'll meet your approval." They entered a side door. Countless servants rushed around carrying a whole list of objects.

Bernard unlocked another door to reveal a lush room. "The dress you asked for will be hanging in the closet, as will the jewels and whatever else was on your list. Is there anything more you require? Feel free to use the phone by the bed. Press one and it will call me directly. Mister Casanova, your room is the next one down." He walked away.

"Alright. What's the plan?" asked Gilbert.

"I'm gonna get ready. Ya gonna sit quietly in ya room." She tried to close the door but he slid his foot in.

"And then what?"

"And then nothing."

"Excuse me?"

"Look, I don't want ya banjo playing, cousin loving, hog wrestling ways mucking things up, ya know? No offense."

Banjo playing? "Offense taken. I'll be fine. Besides, you may need a little help."

"I'm stuck with an idiot," she rubbed her forehead, "this- this is big players. Cartel. Politicians. Royalty. Billionaires. Ya even look at the wrong person and ya blow the whole thing."

"I thought we were partners? And where do you fit into all this? You gonna get every guy to fall for you?"

"Not if ya don't let me get ready." She kicked his foot and slammed the door.

Gilbert went to his own room. Banjo playing? Idiot? What did he hate most? The condescending tone? The lack of faith? The idea of all those eyes devouring her? No. Why should he care?

He laid on the bed and stared at himself in the mirrored ceiling. He could play the part. He could be charming. Be fancy.

Banjo playing? Banjo playing? He wasn't even that country! Maybe that's what the party needed. A little country. And in the process he could prove he wasn't useless.

Gilbert rolled over, picked up the phone, and hit one.

"Evening, sir. What can I do for you?"

"Bernard. Y'all have any fancy clothes that might fit?"

18 ... Lost

Hours later Gilbert emerged with stiff legs and the stench of sweat and perfume and something else he was certain would never come off burned deep into his skin. He reached for support and put his full weight on the balcony.

"Oh, that was fun, wasn't it?" Caroline came up behind him and threw her arms around his neck. He made no move to encourage or dissuade her. She ran a smooth finger along his chin and softly kissed his lips. "So I'll see you around? Gilbert? Gilbert? Hello? Anyone home?"

Sleep. He wanted to fall asleep and never wake up.

19 ... Eyes of God

The homeless man snoring in the pew directly behind Gilbert reminded him of the one who came to mass growing up. Even had a similar scar running across his face. What was his name? Red? Terry? Maybe Red was just a nickname, and Terry his legal? The last Gilbert saw of the man was a decade earlier when the congregation chased the poor fellow out.

Then there was the time a priest yelled at a family for failing to quiet a crying child. Thinking back, the mother couldn't have been much older than him now. Definitely under thirty. Did people actually stand and clap? He shifted uncomfortably. It was embarrassing, and ironically amusing, how a religion built on simplicity and love could be so cruel and complicated.

He turned forward and felt the murals of Saints Peter and Paul burning into his soul. How much money went into this place? The cathedral could easily fit a thousand, maybe more. High heels clicked along granite floors and children rolled chubby faces at white marble columns and the golden ceiling. Various verses and phrases were carved in bronze letters: *DO ONTO OTHERS, LAMB OF GOD, HE IS RISEN,* and so on. In the center hung an intricate silver-plated crucifix held by four decorative chains. Below that, a rectangular gray altar.

Out of the corner of his eye he watched Angela busy herself with making weird faces. Her audience, a curly haired toddler, smiled as if it were the funniest thing in the world. She stopped when she noticed Gilbert.

"What? Ya got a problem?"

"No. Just think it's cute."

"Screw off." They fell silent. A minute later Angela kicked his shin. "People are staring at us."

"Don't think Henley's, jeans, and guns exactly meet the dress code."

"Oh and layers of makeup do? Ya god wore a robe and sandals and walked around with a sword. And wasn't white. No, them two. A few rows ahead. Frankenstein and middle-aged Bobby Sue."

He followed her eyes to a miserable looking couple. Every few seconds the lady would glance in their direction then dart back, her dyed blonde hair bobbing as she moved. Gilbert tried to discreetly get a read.

Too late.

With robotic precision the couple stood and exited their pew. Frankenstein shuffled behind his wife. What a giant. In contrast to the hulking and depressed figure, the squat lady rocked her hips and possessed a wide, pink lipped smile. Gilbert didn't need to look closely to see where skin began and makeup ended.

"Hey there! I'm Mary Beth." It was one of the thickest southern accents he'd ever heard. "This here's my husband Daniel. We just wanted to say hello cause we've never seen y'all here before."

Daniel grunted.

Gilbert extended his hand. "Nice to meet y'all. I'm Curtis Canyon. This is my girlfriend—"

"Jericho," said Angela sweetly. "I keep telling this one ta let me introduce us for once."

"Bless your heart, that is such a unique name. And such an interesting choice of outfit. I wish I was that confident. Now, what brings y'all to our little slice of heaven?"

He groaned internally. "Well, we just moved here—"

"Oh, so y'all are engaged?"

"No, but—"

"Y'all live separately, right?"

Angela hooked her arm under his and laughed a little too loud. "Nope."

Mary Beth's face turned bright red. "Well, don't let us hold you. It was very nice to meet y'all. A little advice, from folks who've been 'round here a while, best not to go 'round saying all that. Alright? Alright."

"Ya been around a while? Then ya must know so much about the church?"

"Well, I don't like to brag but…"

While Mary Beth excitedly detailed the building's history, Gilbert watched her husband. Aside from the occasional nod or word of agreement, the man was a statue. There was more life in a corpse.

"Watch any football?" Gilbert asked.

"No."

Mary Beth cut in. "You'll have to excuse Danny. He doesn't talk much. He travels all over the world for work and likes to relax when home."

"That's interesting. What do ya do? Finance? Sales?"

"Collector," he said icily. "Fine arts and such."

The organ boomed.

"Oh, here we go! It was so nice to meet y'all. I hope to see you on Tuesday." Daniel stared at Gilbert for a few seconds before following his wife back to their seats.

"Did the guy give you a weird feeling? And want me to start calling you Jerry?"

"Never call me that. Ever. It's— never mind. And a bit. Look, word's bound ta get out that we're here and after that who knows. Hell, could already be someone watching us."

"Caroline said she'd stay quiet."

Angela raised an eyebrow. "Keep an eye on Frank."

He filed the information for later processing. "Learn anything?"

"Well," she dramatically threw her head, "the women meet on Tuesdays ta discuss the good word and — *gossip* — scandalous, I know. The men meet on Wednesdays. She made her thoughts known on our lil co-habitation, and, drum roll please, there's a series of old tunnels beneath the building. Access through the altar."

Gilbert smiled at the thought of Angela Bronte sitting and sipping red wine with a group of middle-class suburban women, debating the weekly passive aggressive drama. He gave her three minutes before she snapped. "Feels a little surprising to be sharing that so freely."

"Here's the thing: it's not a secret. 'parently kids sneak down all the time."

"So the treasure might be gone?"

"Nah, doubt it. We would've heard something by now, ya know."

The priest started the service by welcoming the congregation. Gilbert enjoyed the boring familiarity of it all. Deep, monotone, off key singing. Scriptures taken out of context. Moms glancing around, raising their noses at this or that. Fathers checking phones and occasionally swatting bickering siblings.

"Ya do this every week?"

"Used to. Been five or so years. Growing up I went to a Catholic school. Church three times a week and religion class. Got old after a while."

"I'll start praying ta ya, oh pious one. Why'd ya stop?"

The congregation stood.

"Number of reasons. There's this part where everyone stands and hold hands and pray. Supposed to be this moment of community. Dad and I were fighting and he refused to hold my hand."

Angela snorted. A number of heads turned.

"At the time it felt like shit. Don't get me wrong, I was a pain, but still. I'll have to tell you some stories sometime." They sat down. "You ever go to church?"

"Ta be honest I'm surprised I didn't burst inta' flames walking in. Mi familia was always too busy. Mama had a thing for a while when I was younger, but that fizzled out. Never knew my dad." She sank back and studied the ceiling. "Ya do confirmation and all that?"

"Yeah. Picked Saint Jude."

"Hmph. Ya strike me more as a Saint Anthony."

When communion came Gilbert was curious to see what Angela would do. To his surprise she lowered to both knees and stuck out her tongue. The priest placed a wafer and continued.

Once the building cleared Angela and Gilbert made their way to the altar. He acted as lookout while Angela ran her hand along the sides.

Click.

With little effort the back collapsed inwards.

20 ... Thousand Feet Below

The air was heavy and smelled of rotted meat. Angela pulled out her phone and shined the light.

"See anything?"

"Ya know, last I checked we've the same number of eyes, so take a wild guess." She pushed past and picked at the wall. "Late seventeen-hundreds. See the splintering on those beams? Place is ready ta collapse."

"Late seventeen-hundreds? Didn't Womack disappear in—" Gilbert jumped and crashed into the ceiling. "Something ran across my foot."

Angela knelt. "Ya mean this?"

A large squirming rat hit Gilbert in the chest. Tiny claws poked through his shirt and dug into his skin. He smacked it away and wiped his hand against his pants.

"Don't. Do. That."

Angela patted his cheek. "Vamos."

Rats. Rats! Why rats? Of course rats. Send him back to La Guerra. At least then he'd know what to expect. What if the creatures bit him? Or moved as a unit to take him down? Diseases? Oh God. What if they decided to duck under his pants and work their way up? He imagined the wormish tails slithering along his thighs. Gilbert quickly stuffed his pants into his socks.

The noises grew the deeper they dove. Squeaks and clicks and chirps and scratches. Gilbert bit his tongue as tiny feet raced over his. In the dim light, walls and floors appeared to move as a weave of hairy lumps. Blood filled Gilbert's mouth. Then vomit. Instantly a horde collapsed around the fresh pile.

"Oh look! Ya made some friends."

"Shut up and keep moving."

"Or what? Ya gonna make me? Hey, wouldn't it be funny if I tripped ya?"

"Move."

"I'm guessing that's a no?"

"Go."

"Ladies first."

"Angela."

"Gilbert."

A rat bit his shoe. "Damnit! Get serious. I don't wanna be down here."

She rolled her eyes and pushed him. "Stop being a baby and —"

SNAP

A door dropped behind them.

Gilbert threw himself into the wood. Dust fell from the ceiling. Again he tried. Not an inch. Walls closed around him. He could hardly breathe.

"What did you do?" His voice rose. "What did you do?"

"Me? Oh don't even. If ya weren't such a coño we wouldn't be in this mess. Oh the rats! The rats! I'm so scared of the rats! The rats ain't the problem. If ya'd just listened ta me, none of this would've happened."

"Shut up. For the love of all that is good, bad, evil, whatever, shut up."

"Ya don't get ta talk ta me like that. Soldiers don't—"

He threw a fist.

"Oh, is that the best ya got?"

She dodged the next two.

"Ya getting closer."

She danced around with a childish grin plastered on her face.

"I can stand still if that helps."

Gilbert yelled and clapped his hands. "Why are you like this?"

Her mouth twitched. "Like what?"

"This! So— So—" Focus. Breathe.

"I'm waiting…"

He dropped his arms.

"No come on! I'm just starting ta have fun."

Any desire to continue vanished. "Good luck finding the key." He returned to the door.

"That's it? Get a lil' scared and ya tuck tail?"

"Yes. Yes, Angela. You're right. I'm tucking tail. I'm just some guy who got scared. Happy?"

"Fears for the weak."

He tried lifting the door.

"Fine. Run. Be my guest, but I ain't coming back for ya, ya know. If there's some other exit, ya on ya own. And forget about the treasure."

He pushed on the wood. Maybe it rolled back?

"Screw ya Casanova."

He listened to Angela's footsteps fade down the tunnel and out of his life.

Minutes later the door gave.

Maybe he could hitchhike his way back to Knoxville and beg for his old job. They'd been trying to hire young people. Heck, most engineering firms were looking for help. It was an idea. A solid one at least. Get back to work. Get back to hanging with friends. Get back to the way things should be. Career. Family. Grow old and be forgotten. Just waste away with regret, knowing he'd come so close but quit. All his dreams right there. Right freaking there.

He stopped walking and looked over his shoulder.

Right there.

No. He was done. Adventuring wasn't in the cards for him. He gambled and lost. And that girl…she wasn't worth it. The way she treated him. Gilbert took a deep breath and tried to bury it all.

Pop! Pop!

Muffled screams made their way through the darkness.

21 ... The Invisible Enemy

Gilbert listened for anything other than screeching and scratching. He counted.

One. Nothing. Two. Nothing. Three. Nothing. Four. Nothing. Five. Nothing. Six. Nothing. Seve-

Successive shots rang out.

His limbs began to shake. She was a professional. She'd be fine. Two more shots. He groaned. Why didn't his legs work? The world swirled. Gilbert felt as if he was stuck in the waking moments following a deep sleep, when one was not sure who was what or what was where or where the line between life began and dreams ended. He took a step back.

Damnit.

Gilbert vaulted into the shadows, crashing into walls and ignoring the crunching squeals under his feet. Maybe she disturbed a creature or fell into a trap. But the gun shots? The screaming? Her warning from earlier flashed across his mind. What if others already knew their plans? What if they were waiting for them? Damnit, Caroline. Why didn't he just leave? Why didn't he go with her?

The screaming grew louder.

"Ya not real! Ya not real!"

To hell with his own safety. "Angela!"

The smell. The air. It was like swallowing smoke.

The tunnel erupted into a dome of blues, purples, and whites. Black flowers wrapped around thick columns. Charred human remains laid about, gnawed to the bone from years of use. A single beam of light shined on the center where a small stand held a golden wedge. Large letters projected out from it:

EEHEEOEPCESTIWALISACIEOE

NIWSVTLEAHIRRAERTNHELHDR

EMDTKENSUNROTEYEFYSDEBOE

AFOORANLNWWWEUITBUMANOAT

Gilbert slid behind a column. Where was she? And where was the other? He snuck a glance. On the far side of the room was a shaking, huddled mess of orange.

"Angela?"

She gave no reply save for repeating the same hushed phrase over and over.

"Angela? Where are they? Talk to me!" What did they do to her? He tried to steady his hands. Whoever he was up against would surely be a better shot. He'd have a single window. Two if lucky. Gilbert inched around the column and fired.

Pop!

A rat scurried away. His lungs burned as he waited for the return. There was only so much room to hide. How did they get the jump on her? Better yet, how did they get ahead?

"Hey!" Gilbert's voice echoed off the walls. "Come on out!" His heart hummed beneath his ribcage. "It's over!"

"Ya not real. Ya not real. Ya not real." Angela continued to rock and mutter. "Ya not real. Ya not real. Ya not real."

What were they waiting for? They could've easily taken them both already. The bastards were torturing them. Unless...

His stomach caught fire.

This was a prank. To get back at him for before. She knew he'd come running. Gilbert walked across the room. "Alright." He reached out. "Jokes over. You got me."

On contact Angela's body began to violently shake. An animalistic screech sounded. He let go and watched through horrified eyes as she gradually returned to rocking. Her arm was wet.

Her entire body was drenched. Beads of sweat ran down her face.

"Angela?" Gilbert slowly approached. She kicked at the ground, propelling herself away.

"Ya not real. Ya not real. Ya not real."

"Angela, it's me, Gilbert."

"Ya not real. Ya not real. Ya not real."

"I'm sorry about before. I don't know what happened. You got on my nerves, that's all."

She continued to push away. Desperation entered his voice. "I promise it won't happen again. Just knock it off, alright? It's not funny anymore."

"Ya not real. Ya not real. Ya not real."

"I am real!" He grabbed her shoulders.

"No! I don't wanna go!" She started to convulse.

Tears blurred his vision. What was happening? What was this? He had to wake up. He had to wake up.

"Mama!"

Her body went limp.

"No no no." He placed a hand on her chest. Her heart pulsed unlike anything he knew. Sweat pooled. Her skin was scalding.

Gilbert let out a terrified cry of confusion and cradled her head. "H- Help! Somebody!" She was getting hotter. "What do I do? What do I do!"

The surface. She would kill him if he asked for help, but what choice did he have? He laid her down. "St- Stay here. Don't move, okay. Don't move. I'll be right back. You're gonna be okay. Don't move."

Gilbert raced to the pedestal and grabbed the key.

An aged groan shook the room and the stand slowly revolved beneath the floor.

Then stillness.

He focused his ears. The sound was hardly perceptible. Maybe just his imagination. Yes. No. A collective squeal rose out of the darkness. Thousands of tiny feet bulleted past, click-click-clicking on the hard floor. The air grew hot. Unbearably hot. The ground shifted.

Crack!

It all began to collapse. The seamless floor split. Gilbert dodged shards of marble. Light poured in.

He picked up Angela and joined the rats. Beams snapped. Dirt chomped at his heels. Every few feet a cry and a crunch came from underfoot.

They'd never make it.

They'd be trapped or crushed.

Food for rats.

No. No!

Gilbert launched their bodies into a crevice. The pressure of a thousand feet weighed down. Thick tails whipped across his face and lips. Teeth bit into his skin. Claws poked and prodded.

He focused on the body intertwined with his.

22 ... A Not so Holy Ghost

"Ice! Ice!"

The priest hurried into the back. Gilbert threw aside the relics decorating the altar and laid Angela down. He felt her head. She was still heating up.

"Hang in there. Hurry!"

"Here." The priest tossed him full bags of ice and a handful of towels.

Gilbert hacked at the frozen chunks until his fingers were numb and bloody. Melted slush snaked over the sides. Nothing was working. There weren't enough towels.

"Sir," the priest took Gilbert's hands, "What's your name?"

He stuttered it out.

"And her's?"

"Angela."

"Alright. Gilbert, you sit down. Let me take care of Angela."

Gilbert fell back on a snapped column and watched the man work. The priest covered her body with a single layer of towels then poured ice over and along her figure followed by another layer of towels that formed a frozen cocoon. The man stepped back and dried his hands on his robe.

"All we can do now is wait for the paramedics. Are you alright? Did anything fall on you?"

Fall on him? He looked around and realized the entire building had taken damage. Broken glass and chunks of roof littered the church. Outside, horns and screams and sirens wailed. Did he do this?

"No. I- I don't think so. I'm fine."

"Are you sure? There's blood on your boots. And your hands."

Gilbert recoiled at the man's touch.

"Easy now Gilbert, it's alright. I'm just trying to help. I need you to relax. My name's Father Donald Creed. Just call me Don. Do me a favor and focus on your breathing."

He did as the man said. Steadily his heart returned to normal and the world stopped spinning. His muscles loosened. The ringing in his ears subsided as well. He could think clearly.

"You guys are lucky." Don knelt and checked Gilbert's hands. "Y'all shouldn't have been down there."

His chest tightened as their eyes met. The priest's disarming voice was betrayed by a calculating stare. The hold on Gilbert's wrist tightened. It took every ounce of discipline to keep from looking at his bag. Or his knife.

"Please, you're not the first couple to sneak below. We catch high schoolers every other week. I've been telling the board for years we need to fill the hole or someone's gonna get hurt. The place is ancient. Then this earthquake rolls through. To be honest, I'm surprised it hadn't caved yet. Just lucky mass was over." He moved to the other hand and wiped the blood away. Each finger was closely examined.

Gilbert exhaled. "My friend was always interested in this place. We were in town and figured why not check it out. I- I think the whole thing spooked her."

"Horrible stuff. You may want to take her to see someone when she's healthy. Trauma can break a person if untreated. I've known people who were completely different after incidents." With a grunt he stood. "You should be alright. I need to go check the rest of the building. Saw a man wandering around. Looked lost. May God watch over you both." Father Don struggled through the field of debris and out the side.

He was alone.

Gilbert stared at the limp body and replayed the scene in his head. Was it spirits? A vengeful God? Poison? Poison seemed most likely, but when did she take it? At the party? One of the guests must've slipped it into her drink. But why did it take so long?

A buzzing sound came from her leg. Gilbert reached into her pocket and took out her phone. It was Layla.

"Where the hell are you?"

"North Carolina. We—"

"Why?"

"The treasure. Angela said you wanted us to start looking."

The line fell silent.

"Hello?"

"Where is she?"

"She's not able to talk at the moment."

"Well tell her to call me. And get back to the island. Now."

She hung up.

His heart started to race again and his blood boiled. He'd been tricked.

Gilbert put the phone back in Angela's pocket.

"No! Get away!"

Ice scattered as Angela twisted on the altar. Gilbert held her down and dodged bits of saliva. She was stronger than he expected.

"Angela. It's me. It's Gilbert."

"Gilbert?" Staggered gasps evened out. "What are ya doing here? How are ya here? Where," her eyes narrowed then widened in fear. A jagged piece of ice shot to his neck. "Promise ya won't tell." Her face warped into a snarl and she pushed harder. He could feel the weapon cutting his skin.

"I promise, I promise." What was he promising?

She released and laid back. Gilbert stepped out of reach and put a hand to his throat. A thin line of blood ran down his palm. "That how you usually say thanks?"

"Thanks? What are ya talking about? And what's with all the ice? And what happened ta the church? Holy crack house Gilby what'd ya do? Know what? Never mind. Did ya get it?"

"In my bag." He watched her. "Layla called."

"What'd the great one have ta sa— oh."

"Yeah."

"Surprise?"

"She lives!" Father Don made his way through the wreckage with hands hidden. Did the priest always have blonde hair? And a scar across his face? "I heard yelling so I came. Did he get what?"

Gilbert introduced the man. "This is Father Don. He helped with the ice. Was telling him how badly you wanted to see the tunnels and then the earthquake hit and you fainted. Started getting real hot so I rushed you up here."

"Always happy to do the Lord's work. Now, what was it you were asking if he got?"

"Nothing," said Angela.

"No please. I insist." The wide smile revealed several crooked teeth.

Angela leaned against Gilbert, letting her arm fall along his leg.

"Dinner reservations," he said. Dinner reservations? Really?

The priest looked unamused. "A little odd to be worrying about dinner reservations, don't you think? It must be quite the restaurant. Where are these…dinner reservations?"

"It was this little French place," said Angela. "I'm forgetting the name."

"I love French food. The soups and breads and meats." The man's eyes remained locked on the pair. "But for the life of me I can't recall too many notable French restaurants in town. Was it *La Belle Helene*?"

"I'm sure it'll come ta us eventually, ya know. Don't want ta take up ya time."

He waved her off. "No no no. Quit that nonsense. Let's see. If not *La Belle Helene*, maybe it was *Les Papilles*?"

"Maybe," said Gilbert.

"Or perhaps *Le Colimacon*?"

"I—"

"*Le Baratin*? *De la Tour*? Come on now I'm doing all the work. There's *L'Assiette*. *Le Cinq*. *Allard*. Any of those sound familiar? No? Maybe it's in the city? *Seb'on*, the place with the little red windows. *Chez Gabrielle*? They serve the best seasonal soup. And the bread? Out of this world. Let's see…oh! Almost forgot about the *Bistro on Belle*. Not pure French. It's that Amer-icanized stuff — New Orleans — always upsets my stomach, but some people like the kick. Am I missing any?" He muttered off the list of names.

Where had Gilbert seen that scar before? "It may have been the third one."

"It may have been none of them because none of them exist." The smile fell and he brought out a gun. "Bit of advice. If you're going to play this game you must be prepared for anything. You must be quick on your feet. You must hesitate only long enough to convince others that what you say is truth. Too long, too short, and the act is up. Trust the wrong person, you wind up dead. Your little partner here could tell you a thing or two about that."

Angela's face turned red.

"Did I hit a nerve, Jericho? Word travels fast. You best hope that's all I hit. Now, I was told to avoid killing you, but accidents happen. My boss, I'm sure she'd understand."

Damn Caroline.

The man took a step closer. "I would hate to shed more blood in God's house, so let's make this easy. Give me the key."

Gilbert looked for a weapon within reach. "Don't know what you're talking about. Must have us confused."

The man rolled his eyes and took another step. "I know who you both are. Did you really think you're the only ones after the treasure?"

"Let's talk this out."

"Let's not. Now," he raised the gun. "Give me the key or els —"

Steel flashed through the air. The priest dropped the gun and clutched his neck. Blood poured out, pooling along the white marble floor.

"Or else what?" Angela mocked while wiping Gilbert's knife on her leg. "Yeah, that's what I thought. Eat a baguette now."

His ears began to ring.

"Reservations? Reservations? That's the best ya could come up with?" She muttered her usual Spanish. "Well, that's that. What's next? Gil? Gil? Gilbert?"

"What? Yeah. Sure. Whatever."

Part 5
Silver

November 26, 2021

23 ... Surprise

Gilbert paced around the room, his eyes darting between Angela and the clock. Layla was due to arrive any moment. He could picture the scene. She'd burst through the door and grab them both by the necks, yelling about how irresponsible they'd been. She'd toss him off the island. Hell, she'd probably turn him over to the authorities. Or Gustav. Oh God she would, wouldn't she? He'd be right back in shit. No. Worse. Gustav wasn't about to forgive him. Why did he even come back?

"Would ya relax?"

"You don't get to talk. You don't get to say anything. Angela...this was my chance. This was my shot. I could finally prove myself, and you just...you just...why? Do you have any idea what I've given up? Any idea what I've had to do? Look at my hand. Look at my face."

"Two extra fingers ain't gonna make ya much prettier."

His blood boiled. "Is everything a joke to you? Do you see me laughing?"

"I could tickle ya if ya want?"

"I'm not ticklish," he snarled. Breathe. Focus. She's trying to get a rise. "I needed this. I left everything. I have nothing."

"And I don't?" Her mouth twitched. "The great Layla London. The fair, all-knowing, kindhearted Layla London. Miss pristine and the queen of clean herself." She started to laugh. "Ya and everyone else are so, so, so freaking cute! So adorable. So- So- Oh! It makes me wanna vomit."

"Don't talk about her like that."

"Why? Ya don't talk about the Butcher all nice and stuff."

"Next time you freak out don't count on any help."

A lamp shot past Gilbert's head and shattered against a wall.

"Oops. It slipped."

Outside Charles began barking.

"Dumb dog. What're ya yelling at now?" She dragged a table to the window and peered out.

Breathe. Focus. Maybe he could make things right. He'd been tricked. It wasn't like he was aiming to break Layla's trust. Well.

132

It wasn't like he was aiming to break Layla's trust again. It was an honest mistake. It wasn't his fault. It was Angela's.

She was still looking out the window.

"Who is it?"

No reply.

He climbed up next to her and saw three black vans parked in front of the bar. A man with a silver shield on his sleeve got out and shot Charles. Two more followed dragging the bruised and bloodied body of Layla London. A fourth he recognized as Auriol Silver, the man he was sold to.

They'd found him.

24 ... Rising Heat

"There is no reasoning with them. And keep ya voice down," Angela hissed. She ripped out drawers and dumped the contents on her bed. Journals, drawings, wooden toys, clothes. She stuffed her bag.

Gilbert's mind raced. What if he found a way to pay whatever it was? Or challenged them to a fight? Or go out guns blazing?

"Where is she?" shouted Auriol.

Pop!

Layla screamed. "Gabrielle and I had an agreement!"

What had he done? Layla was paying for his stupidity. Angela might die. And the town? Maybe he should turn himself in? No. Calm down. Think.

Angela drove an elbow into his throat. "I swear ta whatever god, idol, or magazine ya jerk ta if ya throw up…my plane should be refueled by now. There's an island not far we can get supplies at. Pack ya things."

"What about Layla? We can't just leave her."

"The woman's dead. The whole island is."

More screams.

"Where is she London? Where is Jericho?"

"She's not here! I don't know what you're talking abou—"

Pop!

"There should be a car in the back. Slide the roof. Zip the line. Bob's ya freaking uncle."

"I won't leave her."

"If ya wanna die, be my guest. Otherwise come on."

They slipped onto the roof.

"She's not here! Angela said she left Jericho in the Amazon!"

Pop!

"You're running out of joints."

"Go to hell!"

"Detonarlo!"

The force knocked Gilbert on his back. A boom that could only announce death burst his ears and the earth began to shake. Darkness filled the skies and glowing globs of red, white, yellow, and orange splattered the mountain. The stench of sulfur stung his nose. In the distance a siren began to wail. He locked eyes with Angela. Both scrambled off the roof.

Gilbert jumped into the driver's seat of a rusty jeep and turned the key. With a kick the machine jolted forward as he slammed his foot. The tiny arm dove into the red and the engine howled for its life. Dust clouded the air. They shot past the front of the building. Bullets pinged the body and shattered glass. In the mirror he could see Angela's hair flapping while she returned fire. 70, 75, 80. The black suited assailants were closing in. 85, 90, 95. Metal whizzed past his ear. 100, 105, 110. Could this thing go any faster? 115, 120, 125. Come on, come on! The town was coming up. The jeep shuddered, threatening to disintegrate. Faster! Faster!

"Look out!"

The sound of stretched metal filled his ears as they twisted through the air. He caught snippets of green grass, black skies, red fire. With a jolt and thud and screech he slammed into a wall. Blood rushed to his head. His left arm was in excruciating pain. He crawled through a broken window and tried to make sense of things.

All around him was hell. The sky was hidden. Streets were on fire. Chunks of smoking earth smashed through buildings and exploded into a fiery rain. Gilbert heard shrieks behind blocked doors. Nearby Angela rocked on her side with her ears covered. He shielded himself from the stampede and grabbed her.

Clang!

The bell tower collided with another building. Dust filled the alleys. He couldn't see. He couldn't breathe. Bits of stone tore the insides of his mouth. Shapeless forms ran into him. Where were the docks? Which way was he going? People pushed. Air. Air! Heat rose at his back. The sound of wood replaced the sound of stone.

Flaming wreckage consumed the waters. Gilbert could just make out the shape of Pablo's ship drifting out.

"Pablo!" Damn Angela was heavy. "Pablo!"

He was running out of dock.

The captain launched a life saver. Gripping Angela, Gilbert plunged into the waves. He felt the hard plastic.

A handful of strangers pulled them on deck.

"Señor, Miss London?"

Before he could answer Angela tackled him.

"Ya can't tell!" she snarled. Saliva shot from her mouth and her face looked as if it were possessed. "Ya can't tell!"

Was she mad? Don't tell who what? Jagged nails dug into his skin.

Two men rushed over and dragged the kicking woman off.

"Throw the bruja in a cage," ordered the captain.

"NO!" The cry was inhuman. Angela struggled harder. She managed to free a hand and clawed the closest person. Two more men grabbed her legs. The crowd split to let them pass.

Pablo helped him to his feet and nodded. Gilbert looked back at the island on fire.

25 ... The Wild Blue Ocean

"Silence!" yelled Pablo. The room of men stopped arguing.

Gilbert noted the range of emotions. Hope. Fear. Dread. Disgust. They'd been going round for the past two days and this morning was no different.

An older man stepped forward. "When will we go back?"

"Go back?" said another. "Go back to what? You can still see the cloud from here. There's nothing to go back to."

"Then where else can we go? We're nearly out of food and already out of water. We have mouths to feed. Families. Children."

"What about the witch?"

"What about the witch? We haven't been feeding her."

"My wife says she saw food scraps near the cage."

All eyes turned to Gilbert. Did he really have to defend feeding someone? "It's from my own rations. What we're doing isn't right. We need to let her out."

"So she can kill us? You all heard the stories. She eats children. I say we throw 'em both over and be done with it."

Several men nodded.

"We're not throwing anyone over," said the captain. He rubbed his eyes. "What we need to do is not panic and stay together. We could make for La Guerra."

The room groaned.

"My wife's brother visited there and never returned."

"Pablo, do we even have enough supplies to get there? How much do we have left?"

"Two days. Five if we stretch it more than already."

"Two days? It'll take eleven. Are you trying to kill us?"

The room devolved into yelling and screaming.

"Enough. We've been at this for two hours. Meet back in fifteen."

Gilbert shuffled onto the deck. He wet his lips and let the white sun cook his face. How ironic. Surrounded by calm blue waters but going to die of thirst.

He imagined the progression. Slowly he'd dry like an old sponge. His mouth would crack, the thin hard skin acting as a knife while his tongue licked flecks of blood. Every day his skeleton would be more and more pronounced. Would he hallucinate? What would he see? A nice, cool waterfall? Home? Gosh, how he took his old life for granted!

And what about the others? The families?

The fathers would go first. Then the mothers. Then the children. Gilbert always believed if in a situation like this he'd valiantly surrender himself for the less fortunate, whatever that meant. It was an easy thing to say from the comfort of an American suburb. He shook the thoughts from his head and continued to the front of the ship.

Not so discreetly the women shifted themselves between him and the playing children. They all blamed Angela for the disaster. Her brash, combative attitude only fueled suspicions and made for an easy scapegoat. And since Gilbert brought her on board, a few held him equally responsible despite Pablo's assurances. He smiled and politely greeted them in Spanish. Maybe he could prove them wrong. Kill them with kindness, his dad would say.

From a distance the cage looked empty. Only once next to it could he see the figure curled up in the corner. If someone a year ago said he'd witness such a sight he'd have laughed. But here he was. He could vaguely make out the green eyes following his every movement. Angela looked like shit.

"You alright? Here, got you an apple." The fruit bounced off her side and rolled with the ship. "So, being in a cage. Not as much fun as it sounds, is it?" He tried a few more jokes before giving up. "Been hounding Pablo about getting you out. Don't understand what their problem is. Separating you until you cooled off? Okay. Sure. But this? This is just wrong."

Her eyes stayed locked on him.

"You're not actually a witch, right?" What was he saying? The sun must really be doing a number on his brain. "Forget I said that. To be honest things aren't looking good. Water is nearly gone. And sounds like we're going to La Guerra." The words were acid. Someone was bound to recognize him. With any luck he'd die before reaching town. Out of all the islands...

His head shot up. "You mentioned another island, right? A place we could resupply?"

He perceived the slightest nod. Maybe it was just her moving with the boat.

"Is it closer than La Guerra?"

This time there was no doubt.

"How many days? Ten? Eight? Five? Three? Four? Four." An idea formed. If they could make it to the island they may actually survive. They could resupply. Continue their journey. Get home.

"We'd all be safe, right?"

"No." The voice was like dust.

"But it's safer than La Guerra?"

"No."

"You're just saying that because you're mad at everyone?"

"No. They will die."

"So we have to go to La Guerra?"

"Gilbert. La Guerra is too far. Plata is our only choice."

"But you just said—"

"Say we make it. Say by some miracle, by some rabbit out of an ass chance we reach La Guerra alive. They'll kill ya. I bet the Butcher makes a show of it. Long. Slow. Painfully painful. He'll cut ya apart piece by piece. It won't be a day. Or two. Or three. No. I've heard stories that last years. Ya'd lose ya mind. Ya'd be this— this— animal. This naked, scared, hunched over animal. Scurrying shadow ta shadow. Chirps and squeals and screams. And the rest of us? Well, if we did make it, which we won't, we'd be slaves. The men would be killed. The women sold off ta evil. The children probably worse. But if we go ta Plata, we might make it. We might live. We might find the treasure. We— We— We can help rebuild Dorado or whatever ya want ta do."

"And the others? The families? The kids?"

"There's too many."

"There's gotta be a way."

"If we get caught…they're already dead. Don't get ya'self — don't get us killed. Ya can't save 'em all, but ya can save two."

She had to be overreacting. If he was thrown in a cage he'd probably be the same. And who'd turn down starving, helpless people?

"I'll get you out. Wait here." He rejoined the others in the cabin.

Pablo stepped forward. "I think La Guerra is our only option. We'll have to cut rations, but I believe—"

"Excuse me," said Gilbert, "I have an idea."

"Oh! The witch's pet wants to speak."

"Tella. Señor?"

Breathe. "Before, well, before everything, Layla was planning on sending Angela and I on a mission. We were going to stop at a nearby island — one that's closer than La Guerra — and resupply. Angela knows where the island is."

"Who's Angela?"

"Girl in the cage."

A chill ran through the room.

"Young man, how much closer?"

"Four days."

"That might just work."

"We could do that!"

"No," said the captain. "Not there. We head for La Guerra."

"Pablo, we all trust you. But four days?"

"Guido. That island is bad news."

"Worse than La Guerra? What choice do we have?"

"How can you all even consider this?" asked Tella. "The words of a witch's pet?"

"Layla never led us wrong before. Did she really plan this? What was she sending you after?"

Gilbert took out the journal and held it up. "We're after the Pirate Womack's treasure. I can't guarantee anything, but if we go to the island I'm sure we can find help. Maybe even continue searching for the treasure. We could use some to rebuild Dorado."

"That island is evil."

"Pablo. We stop by, restock, then head to La Guerra. Send a small group ashore, not the whole ship. Heading straight to Gustav with nothing is suicide. I'm willing to bet he's heard what happened and is waiting for any survivors. Boy, Gilbert, isn't it? You said the girl knows?"

"Aye."

"And I take it she won't speak unless freed?"

"Aye."

"Pablo?"

The captain sighed. "This is a mistake."

"I say we put it to a vote. All those in favor of La Guerra?"

Four men raised their hands.

"All those in favor of the witch?"

A dozen hands went up.

Pablo walked across the room and handed Gilbert a key. "If they die, it's on you."

The piece of metal felt heavy.

"She'll kill every last one of us," yelled Tella. "She'll eat the children! Just find out the location then throw them both in the sea!"

Gilbert ignored the man and unlocked the cage. He offered his hand to Angela. Her body tensed. Like a frightened animal she scrambled out, jolting the cage. Her head snapped from right to left. Her fingers looked like claws. Each breath was quick and harsh.

"See! Look at her. She'll kill us and eat us."

Her demeanor changed. She straightened, stretched, and let out a shrill whistle that sliced through the air.

"No no no. Ya see, people are way too chewy, ya know. Way too chewy. All the bones and skin and hair. Yuck. Pain in the ass ta pass. But I hear sharks love short little fat men."

"Is- Is that a threat?"

"Call me a witch again and find out."

"Enough." Pablo stepped between them. "You all have jobs to do. Do it." The crowd dispersed. "You two, with me."

26 ... Trouble in Paradise

Pablo scratched his head and paced the small room. Angela told him everything. The journal, the strange men, the eruption. When it came to Gilbert, he left out recognizing Auriol. After pointing out where the island was, she went below for sleep. Gilbert waited until the door shut to ask the question burning his mind.

"What's so bad about the island?"

The captain leaned against the table. "Up until ten years ago all was fine, then suddenly they started going quiet. Any ship that went in never came out. Most people say it's ghosts or spirits or demons or even the tide. Bunch of nonsense. Drug lords and criminals control a number of these places. My guess is someone, some group, came in and set up shop."

147

"Wouldn't the police do something?"

"You have much to learn. The government is as corrupt as the criminals, and still they have the nerve to call themselves saints. I pray this works out, but I'm not holding my breath. Here," he handed Gilbert a pistol, "keep it hidden. I don't trust the girl. Neither should you. If you see anything, don't hesitate."

Gilbert stuffed the weapon in the back of his pants and pulled his shirt over. "After the vote I didn't think you'd want anything to do with me."

"You were right, señor. It wasn't fair to let her stay caged. Everyone here is scared, including me. Sometimes fear makes us do crazy things. We need to keep each other straight. Make sure we don't lose ourselves. Go, get some rest."

He exchanged a few more words and then went to check on Angela. Seven rows of blankets, rags, and whatever else was relatively soft covered the floor. Boxes and sacks were pushed against the walls or hung from nets across the low ceiling. He found Angela in the far corner sharpening a knife.

"I'm guessing ya the one with my bag? Nice of everyone ta give us space."

"Don't think they trust you. Is that my knife?"

"Us. And what gave it away? People avoiding ya? The fact they threw me in a cage? Or maybe, just a thought, it was the fat one wanting ta throw us over the side while people cheered?

148

Wouldn't mind doing that ta him, ya know." She ran her thumb along the knife's edge. "Do ya think if I hit him hard enough candy would come out?"

"What's your problem?"

"How much time ya got? Nah, I just don't like being thrown in another cage or called a witch or a freaking cannibal." She threw the knife. The blade sunk into the metal wall with a low thud. "That'll do. But hey! Here we are."

"Thought you'd be a bit more appreciative I got you out. And kept you fed. And—"

"I'm gonna stop ya right there chief. I am. But I ain't playing the whole damsel in distress bit. Find another girl for that."

"Fair enough. You weren't serious before, right? With Tella?"

She retrieved the knife. "Ya still got the journal? Didn't see it in ya bag."

"Yeah."

"Give it ta me."

He started to reach into his jacket then stopped. "Just remembered I left the book up top."

"I see the outline."

"That's another. Private stuff."

"No it's not."

"Yeah it is. Notes, thoughts, all that."

"I'm not an idiot, ya know." She pointed the weapon at him. Gilbert made a show of scratching his lower back. Her eyes narrowed. "Don't even think about it."

The soft slapping of waves was deafening.

"Angela, I'm your friend."

"Go."

Gilbert obeyed and returned topside.

What was he doing! Why did he lie? He reached into his jacket and pulled out the journal.

"Hola!" A man grabbed Gilbert's shoulder, knocking the journal free. Before he could blink there was a football field's length between him and where the book landed in the water. "I want to thank you for giving us hope. I thought my wife and I were gonna die for sure. Sorry, did you drop something? Look, if you need anything, anything at all…"

The words went in one ear and out the other. He had it in his hands. Then he didn't. It was there. Now it wasn't. No. No no no. No! Should he jump? They were too far. Damnit! Don't tell Angela. Damnit! Tell her people were talking about it, so he decided not to bring it out. That should do it. It was stolen. Yeah. Maybe he could still piece it all together. Damnit!

The rest of the day was spent agonizing over the loss. Only after dinner did he snap out of it when a young child ran up to Pablo and whispered something in his ear. The man's face fell.

Gilbert realized the only people missing were Angela and Tella.

27 ... The Sound of Justice

Gilbert closed the door to the cabin.

"Everything alright?"

Pablo loaded Angela's revolver. There was no emotion on his face.

"It's Tella," he muttered. "The witch thinks she can take us out? Thinks she can lead better?"

"Let's just calm down a minute."

"No!" The captain swept his arm across the table. Glass shattered. "No, señor. Don't you see what she's doing? The witch is leading us to our deaths. Picking us off one by one. Driving us apart. Turning everyone against me. Think! She's one of them. I know it. She must be. She…" The captain's eyes widened. "Yes.

Of course. It all makes sense. Layla hiding her. The volcano. The island." He grabbed Gilbert and shoved him against a wall. Flecks of yellow spittle shot from his mouth. "You see it, señor? You see it don't you? We have to stop her. We have to stop the madness."

Deep purple sags hung beneath Pablo's cracked eyes. Veins pulsed under dirty skin. And that smell…

"Pablo," Gilbert placed his hands over the captain's. "You're tired. You need sleep. You haven't sat down since everything happened. You're not…you're not thinking straight."

"But I am! I am, señor! It's you that's not. You're letting her in your head. Letting her lead you to die. Why can't you all see it? I'm trying to save you. That island means death." He collapsed to the floor. "I'm trying to save them."

Gilbert glanced outside and saw heads turning. He knelt beside the captain. "We'll be okay. Please, just sleep."

"Why do you support her?" Darkness entered his voice. "Why do you care what happens to this stranger? I pulled you from the sea. I saved you. I vouched for you. I'm the only friend you have, and you…and you…turn on me?"

The man's eyes traveled to the gun sitting on the table.

"You're my friend, Pablo. I'm not turning on you. No one's turning on you. All I'm saying is you're not thinking straight."

"No no no. Things have never been clearer in my life. You fooled my father. You fooled Layla. You nearly fooled me."

"I've done nothing but tell the truth."

"Have you? Layla told me you tried to steal that journal. All of a sudden you show up and it goes to hell. You get the people riled up. Get them wanting to go to that island. It all makes sense."

Gilbert reached for the gun tucked into his pants.

"You need to calm down."

Color returned to the man's face. "Forgive me, señor. Perhaps you are right. Perhaps I am just tired. Go. Let me sleep. We shall talk in the morning."

Gilbert slipped out and headed below. He no longer had an appetite, nor any desire to face the stares and whispers. He made his way through the darkness and found his spot. Angela was curled up in the corner, her bag protected by her body.

He placed his gun underneath his pillow and laid down and closed his eyes. Physically, he was the most exhausted he'd ever been. His mind was a different story. The captain's words waged war. Was the woman sleeping beside him really one of the slavers or mercenaries or whatever the hell they were? Was she leading them all to their deaths? Surely he was smart enough to recognize the signs, if there were any. No. She couldn't be. Everyone was tired. On edge. And this 'witch' nonsense? Tella was a drunk who probably fell overboard. Terrible business, but not murder. Angela was weird. That was all. And he wasn't turning on Pablo, just trying to keep evil at bay and speak reason. He had to keep them together long enough to reach the island.

The sound of metal on metal tore him from his thoughts. Gilbert opened an eye to see the door close. Footsteps – far too slow and careful – made their way down the stairs and across the room. A shadow stopped over Angela.

"You won't plague us any longer." The shadow reached for something.

Gilbert grabbed his gun and fired.

28 ... The Gates of Hell

Angela Bronte's face was dried black with the captain's blood.

It'd been four days. Tiny cracks ran along her forehead, her cheeks, her eyes — wherever the face stretched while smiling. Gilbert gave up trying to convince her to wipe it off. Maybe she hated water. Maybe she was crazy. She was probably crazy. With a grin she'd insist it was good for the skin. What a lousy lie.

In silence their little orange raft floated through a maze of jagged rocks that threatened to rip it all to shreds. The shadows of the looming island cast an ominous presence, as if it were the entrance to evil herself. The remains of their boat sat sinking a mile out in a bubbling pool of mangled metal. Black creatures circled beneath the water's surface having caught the scent of death off twenty bodies.

Gilbert struggled to calm his hands. "We shouldn't have killed the kids."

Angela rolled her head. "Not this again. Would ya lighten up? What're we gonna do, bring 'em? We didn't know 'em. And besides, they'd've just slowed us down or given us away. They got it easy." She crawled over. "Gilby. Look at me. Move on. Mama values her privacy. If ya no use, ya dead. I've seen the things she's done. We once got a guy ta kill his best friend by threatening his family. And this other time…"

Gilbert knew she was right. After he learned the true nature of the island, of Angela, in a twisted way what she did was mercy. He still hated it. "How exactly do we make it through?"

"Well, nothing happens here without her knowing. No one in, and definitely nothing out. But…"

"You know how."

She fired a finger gun. "Bingo dingo."

They pulled the raft onto the sand and started cutting it apart, burying the pieces and covering their tracks with heavy leaves. There was no going back. Angela took lead and they began climbing. After eight grueling miles uphill Gilbert wanted to die. He could hike for days, but each step birthed a new breed of pain and the steady pace they started with ground to a crawl. His heart screamed with every labored pulse, and his head throbbed as if being pinched above the neck with railroad spikes.

Angela stopped to catch her breath and inhaled the silence. "Holy whore in a church. Forgot how much I hated this. Damn what a climb." Tossing her bag aside and collapsing on the red earth, she allowed herself to go limp. "Ya know, I used ta come up here a lot. Can't beat the views."

From their height the mountains faded from a mosaic of blacks, reds, blues, and whites to sprawling greens and yellows down in the valley. Large clouds provided shade that highlighted the natural curves and formations. In the center of it all stood a massive rock covered in melting ice that branched to a number of lakes.

"Before Mama got the whole island there was this small village down there. Probably a mile or two away. Sometimes I would visit, ya know. Never learned anyone's names. They would try ta make me laugh or teach me this or that if I would listen." Her hand drifted through the air as if running through the memories. "There was this ritual. Ya'd take coca leaves — coca not coco, big difference — and bring 'em round and round ten or so times and then hold 'em ta ya lips and pray silently. Ask the mountains for passage or some bullshit."

A small pool of blood ringed her thumb nail where she'd been picking. Ever since they took command of the boat something changed. She was more on edge. More vicious. More deter-mined.

He lowered himself to the ground. "What else did they teach?"

"Oh, this and that. Let me think." She rolled to her side and yanked up a clump of tall yellow grass. She twisted the lines to form a rough rope. "They did it a lot better, but ya get the idea." Her eyes lit up. "Did ya know that on the mainland, they twist hundreds of these guys ta make a bridge? I mean. A lotta people think the natives were backwards and uncivilized, but if ya study even a little, ya see that's p'urdy wrong."

Gilbert tried to embrace the moment. He felt like an actual adventurer, learning about cultures in an exotic place with beautiful views and interesting people. For all Angela's terrifying exterior, something was lost on the inside that he intended to uncover. He steadied himself as she continued her lessons. Hopefully the headache burrowing itself into his skull would go away.

"…and that's why ya got the condor, panther, and snake. Ya following? Good." She glanced at her watch. "Break time's over. We'll camp at a lower elevation."

The downhill slide was much more enjoyable. Granite walls rose from crushed red dust, forming a bowl with a small lake at the bottom. The pressure beneath his ears continued to grow. By the time they reached a suitable spot each step made his eyes feel as if someone was pulling them back.

Dinner consisted of boiled water and burnt fish. Gilbert closed his eyes and savored every flavorless bite. The charred meat melted on his tongue. Juice streamed from the corners of Angela's lips. Each sip of water was life giving.

"I thought you didn't eat meat."

"I'm telling myself it's bugs." Angela filled her cup with leaves and offered some to Gilbert. "Helps with the altitude."

Gilbert passed. "It's not the altitude. Just tired." He needed to be alert, but every movement was agony. Still, he wouldn't stoop to drugs or witchcraft or whatever it was. He fell onto a sleeping bag, wincing at the slightest shift. If he stayed still enough the pain was only a simmer. Sleep would help. Of course it would. Without a word he closed himself off.

An unusual darkness fell over him. Was this a dream? No, how could it be? His thoughts were still clear. Cool water rushed along his feet. Moments ago he was on the island. As he crept forward the world spun.

He was home. The boring living room was easily recognizable, but the couches were overturned. The red carpet sat in decay. Roaches crept out from the floor and scurried up the walls. The only things not out of place were the numerous pictures. He took down the family portrait hanging above the fireplace and studied it. Father, mother, brothers, sister. No Gilbert. Just empty space where he should've been.

A high-pitched wail cut the silence.

Gilbert returned the picture and listened. There it was again. The sound came from a closet. Wood rattled, almost breathing. A chill curled up his spine. He reached for the handle.

The door burst open, flinging Gilbert through the air and into a field of wheat. Cautiously he rose then quickly dropped. Tall, slender, creatures robed in shadows with blurred white face huddled a few feet away. The smell of sewage snaked out and attacked his nose. In a pained whisper they spoke. "You abandoned us. You left us to die."

Gilbert tried to control his breathing. They couldn't have seen him.

"But we do, Gilbert. We do see you hiding. We see everything. Always running." Their voices began to rise. "You abandoned us. You threw us to the side. You allowed us to rot into nothingness. We needed you and you ran."

"This isn't real," he whispered. "Wake up."

The circle split with a screech. A black coffin sat open in the center. "Shame."

He felt a pull.

"Shame."

His body was dragged through the dirt.

"Shame."

He picked up speed. Gilbert clawed at the ground.

"Shame!"

Gilbert was thrown into the coffin and the lid slammed shut. He kicked, tossing his body against the sides. The air grew thin. Was he dying? Was this how it ended?

The box lurched and fell, sending Gilbert rolling across the ground into a hard steel wall. Warm water soaked his clothes and stuck to his hands.

The floor shifted steadily back and forth. The room was dark save for a single beam of moonlight falling on a rusty switch. Gilbert slogged through the rising water, stumbling over floating sacks. By the time he reached the other side he was waist deep.

Lights flashed. His eyes adjusted, and with it two realizations: the sacks were bodies, and the water was blood.

Twenty corpses thrashed about. His body refused to listen. Move, damnit! They were almost on him. Raw, cold flesh tore at his clothes. All he could do was watch as they pulled him under. Deeper. Deeper. Deeper.

A rough hand reached through and pulled him out.

Gilbert struggled for air. The room was gone, replaced by the deck of a boat. Four child sized skeletons walked past without a glance. A lone figure in a dull red sweater stood at the bow watching the sea.

"How you doing Gil?" The man said warmly.

"John?" Gilbert's voice was a squeak. "How? I thought—What are you doing here?"

"Oh don't worry about that. How are you? It's been a while." His old friend let out a laugh and smiled with all his teeth. He walked over to a chair and collapsed with a sigh. "Take a seat." Together they watched the ship rock in calm black waters.

"So how ya doing? A little far from home?"

"You have no idea. We're near some compound."

John looked at him with pity. "And then what?"

"I don't know. Part of me wants to go home. But there's this treasure—"

"Treasure? Come on. We both know you don't care about money."

"It's not any treasure. It's this legendary treasure that—"

"So it's still treasure? Does it bring people back from the dead or something?"

"No, but…no. I just want to find it."

"Alright then. What's the plan? What makes you think you can find it?"

"I- I don't know."

"Oh Gilbert Gilbert Gilbert," John chuckled. "No plan. No home. No future. Always on the run. What would your dad say? What would your mom think? Even as a kid you were like this.

Everywhere you go, something bad keeps happening. People keep dying. Things get destroyed. Why keep going? For her? Is she really worth it? How many lives have you ruined? How many more will you destroy? One? One hundred? One thousand? One hundred thousand? What about all those people on that island? You took their homes, their families. And the ship?" John stood and walked back to the railing. "It's a slippery slope. You're like a son to me. I…I don't want you to end up with a bullet in your chest. I don't want you to end up dead or betrayed or whatever. I don't want you to lose who you are."

"I won't. I never meant for any of this. I just wanted…You have to believe me, John. Please. All of this, it's just…unfortunate I guess."

"Unfortunate? Come on, be serious. Eventually you'll reach the end. You can't run forever. You have to face the truth."

Suddenly Gilbert was alone.

A warmth washed over him. Off in the ocean a golden orb hovered just above the surface. It called out, singing in some foreign tongue. He took a step towards it. Something felt off. "Where am I? What is this?" He fought against its pull. The orb began to grow, the light consuming everything in its path.

His eyes shot open. A woman, her face streaked in tears and blood, sung softly and massaged his head.

"Drink."

She handed him a cup filled with brownish-green water and leaves. Without hesitation he swallowed. The hot water refreshed his dry throat, and slowly it all came back.

Angela smiled. "Yeah. Mister 'altitude-got-nothing-on-me' my ass." She let his head drop. "Going crazy ain't as much fun as it sounds, innit. So, what'd'ya see?"

He rolled out of her lap. "I'd rather not." He wanted to forget the whole incident.

"Oh come on," she teased. "I pinkie promise I won't tell."

Gilbert flexed the bandaged wound. "Please stop."

"Uh oh. Somebody's got some skeletons in their closet. Care ta compare?" She started laughing and walked around the fire and got into her bag. "Go choke on a rock. If ya screw up tomorrow, I'm leaving ya."

Gilbert turned away and watched the lights of Silver's compound dance over the hill.

29 ... Cooked Goose

The double-storied building appeared as a dark 'A' against blankets of green. Six guard towers connected by tall, wired fences lined the perimeter. Each was manned by two soldiers and a large gun.

Angela pointed to the greenery. "The highest quality fake plants money can buy. Asked mama once if I could grow a fern. Maybe it was a potato? No, it was a fern. Said something about how 'precious' water was. Bunch of baloney. We filter right out the ocean."

"How's that possible?"

"Dunno. Don't care. Everything's concentrated. Solar panels over that hill. Produce over there. They moved livestock right before I left. Loved messing with the cows." She crawled over Gilbert. "See the two wings there? They lead down ta a bunch of tunnels. I'm talking garages, barracks, storage, and, wait for it… sewage."

He continued staring through the binoculars. "Will we be able to fit?"

"Unless she tore up the whole place in the past eight months and rebuilt, yeah. Plus the system was designed as an escape route if anything unsavory happened." She twisted Gilbert's head to a black lake. A concrete line jutted out nearby.

It all seemed too easy. An operation this big, this secret…why leave something like that so vulnerable? He voiced his thoughts.

"Well, for starters, it's not like we get a ton of visitors. And historically speaking there were security bars. Kinda torched those when I split."

"Why did you split?"

"Slight disagreement between Mama and myself regarding her daughter." She patted his back. "Gilby, trust me. I know what I'm doing. This ain't my first ro-day-oh, aight."

He sat back. "And you're certain it leads to the hangers?"

"Do ya have a better idea? Vamos."

They shouldered their bags and headed for the opening. Clumps of brown liquid sludged out. It smelt like hell. Inside, the tunnel stretched indefinitely.

"Follow every step I take. Might be traps of the booby persuasion." She flicked on her light.

The slick walls were large enough that they only needed to hunch. For miles they waded through putrid gunk. Angela's breakfast went first, then Gilbert's. God, it was awful. He found himself half-walking and half-dreaming. What kind of person was this 'Mama' to afford something so intricate? Better yet, what dangerous things occurred between Angela and her daughter to force Angela to run? Was there a fight? Was it love?

Angela froze. "Do ya hear that?"

He strained his ears. Drops of water clicked against the floor. Waste plopped to the ground. A low hum was barely discernible. It all felt eerie, like someone was watching them.

Angela ran her hand along the walls, the light casting a shadow on her pale face. A thin line of discoloration split the pipe. "Ah poop. I think—"

Crack!

The chamber sprang to life. Doors slammed on either side, throwing him into complete darkness.

"Angela!" he yelled. He started kicking steel. Nothing. He slapped the wall and cursed her for being so arrogant. Of course security would be upgraded. If she would just think.

He shut his eyes to block out the darkness. Breathe. Focus. Breathe. This had to be a dream. It had to be. Horrible, very real, but still a dream. Only months ago his biggest concerns were calculations and why the lady he was flirting with suddenly stopped. He flexed his fingers. No, this was not a dream.

He tried to order his thoughts. Worrying would do him no good. Angela was capable of handling whatever was thrown her way. He had to handle himself. He listened for the hum. At this depth, in these pipes, sound shouldn't flow unless there was an opening.

Steamy residue wormed along his hands and beneath his shirt as he felt his way. He struggled to control his stomach. Roughly ten feet back his arm shot up. Tapping lightly, the sounds vibrated.

Metal.

The faint hum brought with it a cool draft. Yes, this was the right direction. Rising, he was able to fit by slightly contracting his shoulders and discovered he could climb if he wriggled his body.

Inch by inch he worked himself, but as the sweat accumulated he'd slip and loose more than he gained. Three times he crashed back to the bottom. Soaked in sewage and whatever else washed by, he was forced to peel the clothes from his skin and continue naked. His arms began to cry. Invisible needles pierced his legs and back. Blood was drawn. Gilbert painstakingly fought and held whatever ground he could. When the battle became too great he'd stiffen to slow the descent while his muscles healed to bearable levels. Tears rolled down his face. Spread the legs! Push against the steel! Breathe. Breathe! Ignore the pain. Whatever happens, don't look up. Don't look down. Keep going now!

With much effort Gilbert managed to reach a landing. He collapsed, the floor a welcome relief on his body. Only after a time did it occur how warm the passage felt.

He continued along, the growing noise guiding him through a series of twists and turns. The tunnel slowly tightened. His shoulders dragged against the sides. That heat. That awful, terrible heat. He paused only to scrape the sweat and slime dripping from his face. Degree by degree, he was roasting alive.

As he rounded the final bend, Gilbert recoiled. Invisible fire licked his bare skin. The stench of hot metal clogged in his throat. Each breath was a struggled cough, air scratching the soft internal tissues as it exited the body. Through blurry eyes he could just make out a bright light.

He slammed his fist. The sound echoed over the red buzz of coils. Was this another trap? More bait to bring him deeper? He kicked the wall in frustration. What choice did he have? Going back invited a slow, undignified death. He would gradually starve until suppressed instincts took over, forcing him to eat whatever lumps floated past. If disease or hunger didn't kill him, he'd be reduced to an animal. No, if this were to be it, he'd not go quietly.

His heart raced and breathing quickened. It will be painful. It will hurt. But it is only heat. Heat — this heat — will not kill. Right? Right. Not if he keeps moving. Not if he fights. Breathe. Focus. Breathe.

With a scream he faced his foe.

Immediately his mind went numb and his body writhed in agony. Wet skin sizzled. His motions became a rugged machine: Palms. Fists. Arms. Chest. Palms. Fists. Arms. Chest. Half a second. Half a second for each. No more. He could spare no more!

Demonic fervor ruled his legs. They crashed about, denting the sides of the metal in an attempt to propel him forward. Smells of seared flesh hooked his nose.

Guttural screams bellowed forth, filling the tunnel. To those Gilbert latched onto. A reminder he was not yet dead.

"Come on!" he shouted. "Come on you bastard! Don't you give up! Come on!" The light was growing. He was fading. "Come on!"

His life flashed before his eyes. All his regrets were plain as day. All his hopes and dreams went up in smoke. What a waste! Stop it! Think clearly! Nearly there!

His arm slipped and Gilbert rolled to his side.

The fresh shock of pain along the spine contracted his muscles, arching his back and sending his head hurtling into the ceiling. His vision clouded.

"No," he cried out. He could hear his tears evaporating. His bare stomach was scorched and sticking to the ground. "Gilbert. Buddy. Not like this. I'm sorry. I'm sorry." He reached for the light.

The tunnel dropped and he spilled out of the oven. Cool air stabbed his skin. A large crowd of darkly dressed individuals surrounded him, cheering and passing money. A man approached Gilbert and kicked until he passed out.

30 ... Professionals

"Well. Bravo. Quite the show you put on, Mister Casanova. Really gave the boys a run for their money."

Gilbert drifted in and out of lifelessness. He felt drained. Weak. His eyes refused to open.

"Hello?" he said softly.

"Are you with us Mister Casanova? Chavez, wake the child."

The air rushed out of his lungs before the blow registered. Trying to shield himself, Gilbert felt loose wire cut into his wrists. A quick jab followed. There was something about the dual blows that stood out. They were calculated. Professional. Accurate. Each successfully fulfilled their purpose: to instill fear. The slimy emotion crawled along his bare spine.

"Are you with us now Mister Casanova?"

The fog began to dissipate. He took stock of his situation. The room looked to be a simple log cabin. Backed into one corner was an old wood stove flanked by eclectic chairs. In another, beneath a painting of the pyramids, stood a lavish chess board with gold and silver pieces. Opposite was a small table where a hulking figure, Chavez he assumed, studied the contents of their retrieved belongings. In the final sat the miserable naked figure of Angela. He could only see her carved back and orange hair caked in wet blood.

Gilbert faintly called out to her, but not even a shiver was returned.

"Fascinating." The smooth feminine voice came from a speaker above the door.

Painfully, Gilbert began to wriggle out of his restraints without drawing attention. Whatever he'd fallen into wouldn't be resolved with a kind word. He needed to buy time to think.

"Too scared to face me yourself?"

"Hardly. I'm dealing with five other interrogations at the moment and yours is the least pressing. But for your own good I'd recommend only speaking when spoken to."

"And if I don't?"

Chavez approached.

Mustering as much force as he could, Gilbert hurled his shoulder into the man's chest. With a crash both crumpled to floor. His raw skin caught fire. Wasting no time he ran to Angela, but the chains wouldn't give.

Chavez caught Gilbert's ankle and yanked down as if it were no more than a rope. Gilbert squirmed, kicking. Blood flowed from Chavez's nose. A string of Spanish was harshly muttered. In one fluid motion his opponent rose and stomped. The air whistled through Gilbert's teeth as his body constricted.

Rolling away, a sense of dread started to grow. He was outmatched by every definition. Gilbert could keep the fight going, but eventually he'd be worn down. In the event he somehow won, then what? It was safe to guess he was inside the compound. His body was faltering without the added weight. No, he'd have to play whatever games they had in store and hope. If he was still alive there was a reason, and therefore he might have a piece of leverage. He relaxed his muscles.

"That's enough. I believe Mister Casanova's seen reason."

Chavez took a final swing across Gilbert's jaw that sent him stumbling into a wall. He reached for support, knocking over the chess board.

"Careful with that. Now, down to business. My name is Gabrielle Silver, but you may refer to me as Madame. You are Gilbert Casanova. From what my people gathered you work for the United States government in an undisclosed capacity. It would also appear you come from a decently wealthy family but were cut out. What a shame. Regardless, we have names and addresses of your kin should you fail to cooperate. Your accomplice was so kind to inform us as to why you are here. In fact, it wasted no time in telling us everything. No torture was needed on that front. The treasure you seek is a myth, but nevertheless Layla London was a respected rival. If she believed in the Black Lily, there's no harm in looking. It spoke of a journal containing all the notes London gathered. After searching you, your belongings, and your boat, no journal has been found. We did find what it called a key. So, where is the journal Mister Casanova?"

There was his leverage. Leaning forward, "Why would I tell you where the book is? Give it to you, we're good as dead."

"My boy," Silver sighed, "I don't need this treasure. As far as money goes, it would be inconsequential to my operations. No, it would make for quite the interesting find, that's all. Yes, if you tell me where it is you will die, but I will make it painless. If you withhold, it will be slow and agonizing. I have clashed with persons far greater than you on far greater endeavors. Now, where is the journal?"

"What if, and hear me out, we make a trade?"

"Chavez."

Gilbert's face contorted into a soundless scream as his body arched in spasms. All over, muscles involuntarily tightened. His jaw locked shut while teeth grinded together. Fingers bored into his palms. Blood slowly streaked down to the floor. He collapsed into a shaking mass.

The brute came close to Gilbert's ear. The mixture of cheap cologne and sweat was nauseating. "This would be a lot easier if you talk. Lot easier." He began to roll up his sleeves.

Gilbert spat in the man's face. The metallic taste lingered on his tongue. Unfazed, Chavez pulled a cloth from his pocket and laughed.

"You are out of your league, child. You will tell us where the journal is, and you will tell us now."

"I- I'd rather not, if it's all the same."

"Are you always this clever?"

He forced a smile.

What little remained in Gilbert's stomach rocketed across the room. Beneath his chair was a puddle of crimson. His thoughts cut in and out. He needed a plan. Now.

"That's enough."

Chavez retreated.

Gilbert's head rolled towards the chess board. It was worth a chance.

"Silver. Madame," whatever her name was, "I have an offer," he struggled for breath, "You seem like a reasonable woman. How about a game of chess? I- I lost the book, but know it inside-out. I can still find the treasure."

The speaker stayed silent. Did she lose interest? Did she call his bluff?

The door opened. In walked a tall woman with a thin and powerful face that had just started to show signs of aging. Hypnotic blue eyes crawled over him, and her smile was both charming and lethal. Her outfit consisted of a dark jumpsuit and a necklace made of irregular emeralds. She crossed over to Angela and covered her with a blanket.

"Mister Casanova, I am Madame Silver."

31 ... Madame Silver

Madame Silver sat and grinned with the confidence of someone who owned the world. "Your accomplice made you out to be weak and spineless. I hoped you weren't merely brawn, but I will withhold my praise. Chavez, leave us."

"Yes, Mother."

She waited until they were alone before pouring a drink and lighting a cigarette. The harsh smoke hung above her head while they set up the pieces.

"You look at me with such disgust. You know, I believe the people we hate most, we hate because we see ourselves in them."

"You blew up an island."

"You make it sound so simple. Guest's move."

179

Gilbert surveyed the field. Steadying his hand, he reached out. *Pawn to E4.* "There were kids. Families. Innocent people that—"

"That all put themselves at risk." She took a long pull and softly blew a smokey gray line towards Gilbert's face. Her lips twisted. "You didn't know?"

It was more statement than question. Gilbert refused to give her any satisfaction and bite the dangling bait. Still, his mind wandered. Was there a mole on the island? Was it Angela? Was it Layla? Maybe Layla was blackmailed into helping this monster and finally said enough. The explosion was retaliation. "I know."

"No you don't." *Pawn to E5.* "If you did you wouldn't look at me like some evil villain. You think you're the hero on this grand little adventure of yours. I guess that makes it the damsel in need of rescue." She sat back and tapped ash into a tray. "How's that working for you?"

Pawn to F4. He stared her down. "So you're the hero?"

"Boy. I have seen countries worship rapists and killers and the whole spectrum of scum just as often as the upright and just. We're all the heroes of our own story." *Pawn to F4.* She took his piece. "Humor me. Let's say you saw a disheveled young lady selling herself on a street corner. Tight red clothes, too much makeup, that whole lifeless look about her. Like most people you'd probably want nothing to do with such a person. You'd think she should be embarrassed. That she should look for a real job. Apply herself. So on, so forth. You'd either pick up the pace and look the other direction. Or maybe you'd slow down and fantasize about all the dirty little things you'd do and never tell anyone." She leaned in and raised an eyebrow. "But maybe you're not like everyone. You ask to hear her story, learn why she does that disgusting, disgusting job."

Bishop to C4.

Queen to H4. "Check."

Already? *King to F1.*

Silver continued. "She's twenty-one. Studied history because she wanted to be a teacher, just like her mother. Great group of friends. Served at shelters on the weekend. Dated the man of her dreams. A rich, handsome, kind young man. They were in love. They talked day and night about buying a small farm where they could raise a family and grow old. Well," *Pawn to B5.* "One thing led to another and she got pregnant. Everyone pushed for an abortion, but life was far too precious in her eyes. And suddenly all those sweet, sweet promises went out the window. Her friends left. Parents disowned her. She fell behind in school and was forced to drop out. And so there she is, twenty-one, scared, alone, with a screaming baby she has no clue how to care for clinging to her hip."

Bishop to B5.

"But she loves that little child. The way those little eyes shine with such a joy and innocence. She'd do anything for it. She took a day job bagging groceries and at night she waited tables. In the brief moments of quiet she buries herself in books because part of her still clings to the hope that maybe if she can right one tiny part of her life, everything will go back to the way it was. But it's still. Not. Enough." *Knight to F6.*

Knight to F3.

She stared coldly at Angela. "Rent is past due. Every night the landlord comes by and bangs on the door yelling for his money. Her baby is crying, hungry, terrified. She's crying, hungry, terrified. She starts to fall apart. All that hard work amounted to nothing. Then one evening some drunk fool offers her five grand to sleep with him. He's handsome enough, decent enough, but she doesn't want to. She'd never stoop that low, it's not who she is. But what choice does she have? She thinks of her starving child. She thinks of the cold winter. One night. Just this once." *Queen to H6.*

Pawn to D3.

Knight to H5.

Knight to H4.

"Decent move. Now, a couple months pass. Soon she's right back in shit. Another man approaches. Then another. Then another. Until one day her boss makes a move. She says no. He wraps his fat fingers around her arm and threatens to fire her. Still, she refuses. Rumors start to spread. She loses bolth her jobs. People start trying to take her child. Everywhere she goes strangers seem to know who she is. What she is. Out of options she calls up the first man and he sets her up on a street corner. Slowly her soul is chipped away, but it's for her child. She won't abandon it. Not like she was." *Queen to G5.*

Knight to F5.

"You sit back after hearing her story. You're intrigued. Here's a bright young woman who cares deeply and works tirelessly but was dealt a bad hand. As it happens, you've been looking for someone with a knack for history, so you offer her a job. Simple research, but it pays well and she'll have food, water, a bed, safety. She jumps at it. She works harder than the rest. They're in it for the money, the fame, the glory. She's in it for survival. For her child. She climbs through the ranks. She becomes your most reliable historian, and you decide to mentor her yourself. Together you lay the foundations for a peaceful business in a sea of murderers. Then one day you lose an envoy. Then another. Then another." Silver forced a pained smile. "Still, she refuses to cross that line. The barbarians are at the gates. All talks have failed. One of them takes her child. Tell me, is it wrong of a mother to do whatever is necessary to save her child? Is it wrong to kill a band of murderers who had the chance to walk away? Who killed her family?" *Pawn to C6.*

Pawn to G4. "Suppose not."

"My thoughts exactly." *Knight to F6.* "She begins training. More attacks come. More of her people die. Suddenly all who's left look to her for guidance. They all become her children. And like any good mother, she defends them. She doesn't agree with everything she does, but for the good of her family she fights. She provides. She projects strength so that no one will even think of hurting them again." Silver raised her chin. "Does that sound like a villain Mister Casanova?"

Rook to G1. "You destroyed an entire island."

Her laugh froze Gilbert's blood. "Did you not hear anything I just said? I don't kill for fun. I'm not a psychopath. Layla London was a self-righteous prick who was smart enough to get others to do her dirty work but too stupid to ignore her own hype." *Pawn to B5.* "She thought she was untouchable and got greedy. Time after time I tried to play nice. I gave her so many chances. All she had to do—," the glass shattered in her fist. Silver closed her eyes and slowed her breathing until the throbbing vein on her forehead disappeared. "Excuse me. All she had to do was follow one little agreement. Don't let that pathetic excuse for a human," she motioned at Angela, "leave the island. Keep the bitch grounded. That was our compromise. Signed. Sealed. Hands shaken. Then just last week I get a call from the Queen of Zane saying a certain somebody was spotted at a party in America. One of my competitors called me directly. Next thing I know, rumors are running rampant inside and outside these walls. People were saying I lost my edge. And maybe I had. Politics and paperwork and sitting behind a desk can do that. Despite the respect and admiration I had for London and her people, to do nothing would invite war. Was destroying the whole island overkill? Yes. But I had to send a message. I had to reminded those in my world exactly who they were dealing with. Exactly who I am. Exactly what I am."

Pawn to H4. "And what about Angela?" His hands grew tight. "What threat is she?"

Silver's eyes never left the board. "Careful now. You amuse me and hold some value, but that value is not as significant as you think. Don't get yourself killed this early in the game." *Queen to G6.* "Still, it may benefit you to know what you're up against. My daughter, Jericho, had done hundreds of assignments. Intimidations, assassinations, appropriations…the list is endless. She was near perfection. She was ready. I was ready."

Gilbert moved. *Pawn to H5.*

"Time is a cruel adversary, Mister Casanova. I may not look it, but I am old. All of this was for my daughter. All the pain and years of suffering. I never wanted her to endure my hardships. These men and women only follow the strong. It was time she learned to lead. To become their new mother. So I sent her and twenty others deep into the rainforests after an artifact." *Queen to G5*. "Only that," she gestured toward Angela, "returned."

Queen to F3. Now things were starting to click. Silver held Angela responsible for her daughter's death.

Knight to G8.

Bishop to F4. Gilbert removed the figure.

Queen to F6. "I believe in second chances. Everyone makes mistakes. But my daughter...my Jericho...that thing bleeding in the corner failed on all accounts, and not just in the Amazon. After the latest fiasco my hand was forced. I had to send a message."

Knight to C3.

Bishop to C5. "Of course she begged to stay, said she'd never fail again. But no. I sentenced her to die in the morning and when morning came, she was gone." Gilbert noticed a slight tremble in her voice.

Knight to D5. "Why not go after her?"

She straightened. "Oh I did. I did alright. I searched the entire world over, only to discover she was in my backyard running errands for the enemy." She slammed the piece down over his pawn. *Queen to B2*.

Gilbert took the rook. *Bishop to D6*.

"Now, I asked Layla to hand her over, but that's when we came to our agreement. I owed her a few favors, and only the two of us knew. But, well, you know how that played out." *Bishop to G1.*

"Why would she come back?" *Pawn to E5.*

"What else would she do? A wife? Please, she'd kill the man. A teacher? She lacks the patience and communication skills. She's arrogant. No filter. Gets in her own way. But in here she finds meaning. In here she has her uses. Everything out there is boring. Lifeless." *Queen to A1.* "Check." She retrieved his rook.

He was being dismantled. *King to E2.*

Knight to A6.

Knight to G7. "Check." His eyes lingered over Angela. He felt pity. "I'd like to make a change to our agreement."

Silver took her pawn. "You won't take any treasure." *King to D8.*

"No. Angela comes to work for you. All is forgiven." *Queen to F6.* "Check."

"And why would I do that?" *Knight to F6.*

"Why waste a willing talent. Sure, whatever happened with your daughter happened, but maybe keep her away like Layla did. You both win."

Silver sat back and closed her eyes. A few minutes passed. "I will allow her back in some capacity. If you win and find the treasure, that is. And in one month."

"One last thing," a thin smile cracked the corner of his mouth. *Bishop to E7.* "Checkmate."

32 ... Land of the Living

Forty-nine. Fifty. Fifty-one.

Gilbert collapsed onto the cool concrete floor. Sweat rolled down his burning arms. He flipped over and did sit-ups until his sides screamed. Then came squats. He concentrated on the small black crack half-way up the barren wall. Finished, he grabbed the towel and gently dabbed his tender skin. The single fluorescent light flickered.

The morning's gauntlet was painful, but not as excruciating as when he started nine days earlier. While his body continued to heal Gilbert busied himself with the mountain of research — maps, letters, references — Silver provided. Most were copies, but the occasional original would surface. If his instincts were correct the treasure sat beneath a range of hills called L'or des Fous roughly sixty miles from John's new home.

The steel door creaked as latches were thrown back. He swallowed. It was too early for lunch. His guard appeared.

"This way sir. Your belongings will be moved momentarily."

Gilbert's bare feet slapped off the stone. He'd been unconscious when they first threw him in the hole, and only now saw the extent of the prison. Low hanging bulbs threateningly illuminated rows of dark numbered doors. Groans echoed from within.

"Wait. Almost forgot," said the guard. They stopped in front of a door marked '52'. "Boss wanted you to see something. Says you know the guy." He placed his thumb on the lock and waited for the red light to turn green. "Mind the smell."

The stench of human feces choked him. Other than a pile of yellowing sheets in the far corner, the room was empty.

"Hold on." The guard banged a stick against the metal frame. "Gustav. You've got company."

The pile of sheets began to shake and what was left of the man once called Gustav the Butcher faced Gilbert. Even the guard winced at the sight.

Where were his eyes? His nose? Ears? Hands?

Tears streamed from empty holes.

Gilbert never liked the man, but this?

"How long do I have to look?"

"Mate, I don't care."

Gilbert stepped out and the door was shut. The image seared into his brain. Was this a twisted gift? Or maybe a threat of things to come? The guard opened another door and Gilbert was blinded by sunlight. As his eyes adjusted, he realized he was still in the main compound.

Countless artifacts lined dark green walls and wide mahogany floors. Painted vases, ancient weapons, hand crafted murals, complete fossils.

"Impressive, no?" said the guard proudly, "I found the raptors in South Africa."

Gilbert tried to hide his intrigue. "Where are you taking me? And where's Angela?"

"You are being moved to a room that will service both."

"So she's alive?"

"Unfortunately. Through here." He was pushed through a pair of thick wooden doors with gold carvings into a spacious library that rose multiple levels. Worn leather chairs surrounded a brick fireplace. "Accommodations are on the second floor. Food will be brought at the usual times. Expect your belongings shortly."

The door slammed and locked.

Gilbert limped up the carpeted stairs and through the maze of shelves. Homer, Hemingway, Stevens, Cicero. Leather bound volumes and rolled up scrolls. Maps and busts. He set to work combing for any information Silver may have missed.

After an hour the door shot open. Two guards tossed the body of Angela Bronte across the floor and left. Gilbert's eyes traveled over the fresh layer of cuts and scars and bandages. It was a vicious work of art. He approached and lightly touched her shoulder.

In a flash he was driven against a wall. Rough hands wrapped around his neck. "Angela…Angela…Stop…" He reached wildly for a weapon. His hands fumbled over the many stacks of leather. There! He swung *Annals of the Holy Roman Empire*.

She squeezed harder, unfazed.

"Enough!" The icy voice crackled over the speakers. Immediately Angela's grip loosened, and she stepped back like a trained Rottweiler. "You both have a job to do. Do it."

Gilbert fell to the floor rubbing his throat. "What is the matter with you people? I saved your life. I saved it damnit!"

Her face went from surprise to pain to indifference in a matter of seconds. Dark blood oozed from under her bandages where the book hit. She lowered herself, bringing her knees against her chest and hands over her ears.

Gilbert's mind cleared. He grabbed a sheet from the scant bed and gently he wrapped her body before falling back against the wall. For half an hour they sat in silence.

"I'm sorry," he whispered.

"Why?"

"Because I hit you with a book."

"No. Shut up. Why are we alive?"

The question caught him off guard. He'd been so focused on his guilt that the more pressing matter was forgotten. "I beat Silver in chess."

"Well pop the freaking champagne. That doesn't help me. I've been blindfolded and forced fed. What are we doing?"

"Made a deal. We have a month to find the treasure and we get to live. Also, you get to come back and work for her." He searched his mind for anything else. "I also lost London's journal. We were at sea and—"

"Shut up." Emerald eyes studied his face. "Ya said I get ta come back here? Mama agreed ta it?"

"Yes."

"Why?"

"Why what?"

"Why are ya helping me?"

"I don't know. Silver said you tried to come back. Also said you sold me out pretty fast. Doesn't take a genius to put two-and-two together. Saw an opportunity to help."

Her body began to shake with laughter. "Now that's funny. Talk about a hoot. I thought I had ya pegged. The whole heart of gold, meek treasure hunter bit?"

"What?"

"And getting all upset when we killed the captain? When we killed the kids?"

"That was you. Not me."

"Stop! Stop!" She wiped tears from her eyes and swallowed gulps of air. A mix of pain and elation filled her face as she struggled to still her body. "Gilfanso, ya surrounded by thieves and killers. Ya can drop the act, ya know. I see through the whole thing. Help me up."

With a grunt she adjusted the blanket and shuffled to a table. "What have ya written so far?"

"Nothing. I figured Silver would kill me if—"

"No. Mama keeps her deals." She picked up a pen. "Start from the start."

"In France I've been looking at—"

"No. The start. What are we after?" Her voice flirted between quizzical and deeming.

"The Pirate Womack's treasure?"

"Bravo. Very good. And who was the Pirate Womack?"

"I don't think that's important."

Angela sighed and massaged her eyes. "Gilby, I don't know how ya hunt for treasure, but ya doing it wrong. What if there's a clue in a name? Or his ship? Or where he spent time? Now, what do we know?"

For the next five days Gilbert and Angela documented the entire life of the legendary rouge.

"I've narrowed down where L'or des Fous might be," he said. "We can borrow horses and ride out. We have the North Carolina key, but I don't think we have enough time to get the Alaskan one. We'll just use dynamite."

"Absolutely not. What if the treasure is deep underground? We'll be buried. Where in Alaska?"

"Some place called Brockton."

"I've heard of that. Small settlement that was lost centuries ago. Alright. Ya head ta France. I'll go ta Brockton. I have a number of contacts that—"

"I'm coming."

"Gilbert, this isn't up for debate."

"No." Gilbert could feel the heat coming off. "I've trusted you since we first met. Look where that got me. I'm coming."

"No? Look at ya. All affirmative. Kinda cute, like a puppy or something. Fine. Ya can come. But if ya screw this up, if ya put one single toe outta line, I'm cutting it off and ya have ta follow every last order. Understand?"

195

Part 6
Alaska

December 23, 2021

33 ... Alaska

Gilbert hadn't seen the sun in five days.

From inside their little cave, the wasteland expanded out into nothingness. Pockets of black rock jutted out of the frozen earth like wolf's teeth. Even the wind echoed the nasty howl. He turned back and sat by the fire.

"Storms starting to die down. Should get moving before another starts."

Angela remained fixated on the burning logs.

"It's not all bad. We got food, clothes, water—"

"I swear ta-ta-ta-ta god, if ya say another word…" she fell silent and continued shivering.

He moved around and shared his blanket. "Brockton can't be far. Would've been nice if your people got us closer."

"Mama says Alaska is off limits, ya know."

"Why do you call her that?"

"She helped raise me." Her jaw clenched. "Damnit Gilbert. I hate the cold."

They needed to keep their minds off the weather, at least until they could start moving again. "Are there any other organizations like Silver's?"

Angela raised an eyebrow. "What exactly do ya think we do?"

"Don't know. Sell weapons and statues and stuff."

"That's nice. We did just that for a bit but ya have ta pay the bills. Have our hands in a lotta cookie jars. Only way ta keep the others in line. But mama prefers just statues and stuff."

"When I was fighting for Gustav, a man named Auriol Silver was going to buy me. Name ring a—"

"No. We don't deal in people." She started to shrink. "Mama wouldn't do that."

He changed topics.

"What about the Queen?"

"Her? Bunch of nut jobs, that whole cult. Ya see a lotta old power coming outta Europe, North Africa, parts of India and China. The Gondis, Barings, Weis, Harkors, Flemmings. There's a long list. Been around for centuries and I guess some are getting their claws in America, but that place is a jungle. Government won't cooperate so ya end up with a ton of little fish instead of a couple whales."

"And South America?"

The fire danced off her eyes and teeth. "Paradise." She leaned against him and lowered her voice. "The cartels know their place. Usually. Mama isn't like the others. She's not paranoid. She knows if they work together, or at least don't kill the other, they can all win. People make the business out ta be this evil monster. Bunch of junk. Us, the cartel, we do more ta help than their little politics. We fund transportation, build wells, create jobs, hospitals…what more do ya want?"

The whole ordeal didn't sit well with Gilbert. Were the benefits worth the cost? He stared outside and pondered the question. An hour later the storm calmed enough to resume their journey. Angela kicked out the fire while he looped a long chord around his waist. After she tied the other end to herself, they set out.

34 ... The Song That Roars

The wind mauled his face.

Just one foot at a time. Don't act silly. Don't lose focus. Breathe. Ignore the cold. Ignore the pain. One foot at a time.

Gilbert felt three sharp pulls on the line and stopped.

There was mild pleasure seeing Angela struggle through the chest deep snow. The bright orange clad figure inched along, ignoring his earlier advice and stepping wherever she thought the ground would hold. For every correct guess there were five that ended in her legs disappearing and a string of curses. He could see tiny, rapid clouds forming in front of her face.

"Keep telling you to step where I step."

Angela raised her middle finger.

The town of Brockton was somewhere in that desolate wasteland. Another day or two and the key would be theirs. Hopefully
they would be in and out before the storm hit, but for that to happen—

"Cold, Gilbert. I'm freaking cold. My feet are cold. My legs
are cold. My ass is cold. And if ya ask me one more damn time
I'll shoot ya."

The icy comment surprised him. "Didn't say anything."

"Yeah ya did. Ya said…" The ski goggles hid her face. "Let's
keep moving."

The wind came across harder, picking up snow and sending it
off in small twisters. Clouds creeped into view, blocking out the
stars. They would have to find shelter soon.

"Why would anyone build a town out here?"

"It's not the worst idea, ya know. Modern settlers didn't come
around until the mid-eighteenth century, so ya only worrying
about native tribes. They tended ta keep ta themselves, and they
didn't really have a great concept of 'money', so ya gold was
safe. Good news if ya running or hiding from the law."

"But why out here? It's not like a ship could get access. Hell,
we had to jump through hoops just to make it this far."

"I actually got a couple theories. One, the rivers and lakes and
bodies of water were different a few centuries ago. The other is
Womack struck gold."

"Doesn't the river freeze over in winter?"

"Might be why it was abandoned." Angela stopped and looked to the sky.

"You know you're not gonna see it with all the clouds, right?"

"I know I know. One can hope, though. I'll probably never be back so fingers crossed. Heard it's supposed ta be beautiful. I thought for sure we were gonna see them in Fairbanks. Even that lady was surprised they weren't appearing."

"You could always go to Iceland."

"Nah."

Gilbert gave her another minute before pressing them to move.

"Any thought about those letters the key shows?"

"If I had ta guess, it's a cipher. Question is, what type and what's the key for the key? Tell me the riddles again."

"Beneath the roots where my lily once grew."

"Which is — was — the church."

"Under ice my heart once warmed."

She waved her arms around. "Found the ice. And the third?"

"The song that roars in my head. Hear it cry out. It wants me dead."

"No idea. But if I had ta guess, the answer is the cipher."

The song that roars? Wants him dead?

"Look out!" Angela threw Gilbert to the ground and opened fire. "Watch my back!"

Gilbert pulled out his gun but couldn't get a grip. The weapon slipped from his hands and disappeared into the snow. "My gun fell!"

"Well find it!" She fired off another shot.

He began to claw the snow. Taking a chance, he looked at who she was aiming at.

"Angela, there's no one there."

"What?"

Angela stopped shooting and shook her head. "What? No. But they were all just- They were all- I swear, Gilbert. I swear I saw them." She sank to the ground and started rocking. "No no no. Not here."

Gilbert's thoughts were interrupted by a train rapidly approaching, or at least something that sounded like one. He could feel the earth around him vibrating, the snow sliding and pulling him along. Looking to his left, a massive white cloud barreled down at them. He tried to pick Angela up.

"We need to move."

"No no no. I saw them, Gilbert."

"Sure you did. Now move."

Angela struggled to her feet.

"Come on. There's a rock not too far away. Come on. Move!"

The avalanche was gaining size. Gilbert raced out ahead.

"We're nearly there." The rock was only a dozen yards away. Gilbert felt the rope go tight.

"Why aren't you moving?" he yelled.

The orange figure silently stood frozen in the snow. He pulled. Maybe he could drag them?

Angela took out a knife and began to cut the line.

"Stop! Angela!"

The cloud was nearly on them. He pulled harder.

Oh no.

The wall slammed into him.

35 ... Unexpected Guests

Air.

Gilbert clawed his way to the surface and swallowed great gulps of freezing air. His throat burned. His ears rang. Everything hurt, and the parts that didn't were too cold or too numb to care. He pulled himself out and rolled to his back.

It was still night. Or was it morning? He checked his watch but found it broken. His phone was dead. Where was his bag?

Angela!

He yanked the line, watching the cord shoot out from underneath. Finally the frayed ends emerged.

"No no no. Angela?" His voice echoed across the snow.

Nothing.

Gilbert slid back into the hole and began digging. She had to be down there. Slush seeped into the cracks of his clothes and boots and gloves, rendering his fingers useless.

"Gilbert?"

He continued digging.

There was a light tap on his shoulder. "Gilbert."

He spun around and was shocked to see the smiling face of John. "What are you doing here? How are you here?"

John laughed, waving him off. "Ah, don't worry about that. Let's get you out of there before you freeze."

"But Angela? She was shooting at something that wasn't there and then this avalanche came and—"

"I know. I know. She probably cut herself free. See the end of the rope? And even if she didn't, you're in no state to keep looking. If you found her, you'd have no strength to do anything. Come on."

Gilbert climbed out and found himself alone. "John?"

"OVER HERE!"

Off in the distance a small figure waved on top of a hill.

"How'd you get out there?"

"Don't worry! Once the storm clears you should be able to see everything!"

Twenty minutes later Gilbert made it to the top. John was sitting, waiting.

"So," John clapped his hands, "How are ya?"

"Nothing seems broken. Side hurts like hell, though."

"No no. How are you? How is Gilbert Casanova?"

"I- I think I'm alright."

"Good good. That's some view, huh? Look at those mountains. Back in college your dad and I would go skiing on mountains just as big."

Gilbert raised an eyebrow.

"Well, maybe not as big."

All Gilbert could do was laugh. "Still don't believe those stories. Never seen Jerome jump, let alone do anything athletic."

"Yeah. No one ever thought he had a career in professional sports."

"He'd say otherwise."

Now John was laughing. "He would, wouldn't he. There was this one time we were walking to lunch and he rolled his ankle on flat ground. On flat ground! Never let him hear the end of it."

"Back when the pandemic started, he asked me to build this planter box. Big old thing. We finally get it set and we're moving it and he pulls a hamstring. Told him he was old."

"Did y'all grow anything?"

"Of course not. Well, some weird looking tomatoes. Tried strawberries. He did manage to grow a single pepper. Never seen him so proud." He smiled at the thought.

"I didn't know you did wood working."

"Picked it up in college because our TV just sat on the ground. Built this entertainment center. Don't get me wrong, it was a piece of crap. Nails poking out. But it held."

"Are you building anything right now?"

"Not recently, but once I get back I want to try building this folding chair I saw in Buenos Aires."

"That'll be cool. That'll be cool. You probably won't get back, though."

"What?"

"I said that sounds good."

They fell silent.

Gilbert looked for something — anything — in the frozen abyss, but the storm was still too strong. He felt John squeeze his shoulder.

"What are you doing out here, Gilbert?"

"Looking for a key."

John shook his head. "No, I mean, what are you doing out here? Not home. Not in Knoxville. On this crazy adventure. This is something professionals do."

"Maybe I'm crazy." Gilbert joked.

"Maybe."

Knoxville sounded so far away. As if home and family and friends were part of some fairytale that wasn't real. Gilbert dug into the recesses of his mind trying to remember why he set out to begin with. As the words formed he realized how stupid it sounded. "Would you believe me if I said I was trying to impress a girl?"

36 ... Before It All Began

Who the hell calls at 7:30 on a Saturday?

Gilbert dug the phone from his pocket and checked the name. Dad. He declined. It was probably a butt dial. Nothing important at least.

Screams rose out of the deteriorating pink house.

Damn. He missed the start. Gilbert quickly made his way through the knee-high grass and up to the dented metal door. He pulled up and out.

"What are you doing! Don't pass it to him! Lionel is wide open!" Ezekiel yelled at the television. The match wasn't even five minutes in and he was already jumping on the couch.

Gilbert followed the smells of bacon to the kitchen where Hooper stood over the stove in a bathrobe.

"Hey Gilbert. How are ya today?"

"Doing well. You? Food smells good."

"Aw thanks. I'm doing great. Made extra if you're hungry. Bout to watch some soccer."

"Son of a bitch! Good pass. Good pass. Gil, how are we?"

"We're good. Where's Chuck?"

"Sock-Man."

"Sock-Man?"

"Sock-Man!" Chuck bounded out of his room wearing nothing but a sock loincloth. He went straight for Ezekiel.

"No. No. Not during soccer," Ezekiel jumped to the other couch.

Gilbert took a seat. "What do y'all got going on today?"

"Hanging with the old ball and chain," said Chuck while slipping on pants, "Jane and I are grabbing lunch with her parents."

"Z?"

"Alex."

"Hoop?"

"I'm with Abbie."

It was bittersweet. Gilbert's three closest friends were entrenched in fantastic relationships, leaving him the odd man out.

Hooper already proposed, and the other two had been talking about rings in recent weeks.

"What about you? Any big plans?" asked Chuck.

"If you're gonna talk don't do it here. Wait till the half."

They continued. "Not sure. Met some guy hiking who told me where to find the best burger. Still need to clean the apartment. World's my oyster."

"Didn't you just go on a date?"

A sly smile broke Gilbert's face. Chuck's eyes lit up. "Really? Who?"

"I wouldn't exactly call it a date."

"Gil," Ezekiel kept his eyes on the game, "two single people who've expressed interest in each other hanging out for the whole day is a date."

"Who is it?"

"Take a wild guess," said Ezekiel.

"Is it that girl on you team?" Gilbert's smile answered. "No! Haven't you asked out everyone?"

It was an exaggeration, but well founded. "No. Not everyone. Went out with Shanna for a minute. It's Rebecca."

"You were on Diane for a while."

"What about Alyssa?"

He tried to defend himself. "She's on another team, alright. And I've said it before, where I work I don't exactly meet a lot of prospects. Old, white, and male isn't my type."

"Rebecca's white. So is Shanna. What'd y'all do? Another hike?"

"Yes."

The room booed.

"Guy's a one trick pony."

His voice rose in pitch. "It's a good date. Plenty of time to talk. You're moving, see—"

"Gil, your definition of an easy hike is twenty miles with a bunch of bears."

"That was one time."

"What did y'all talk about?"

"Well, I picked her up about seven o'clock—"

"In the morning?"

"In the morning, and we drive to the trail. So we start walking — oh, on the drive over I got to show her my photo book—"

"That just happened to be in your car?"

Gilbert shrugged. "All I'm saying is she loved the pictures. But we're walking and it's perfect. Snow's everywhere, not too many people, a little cold but not too cold. We get a quarter of the way up and she starts talking about how hard it is—"

"How far were y'all?"

"About two-and-a-half, three miles. Not that far. And I'm like, 'Hey, trust me, it'll be worth it', so she says okay. We have a little snowball fight. She's telling me about her roommates, her family, what she wants to do after college. Funny thing. We're asking each other where our dream house would be, and she was so excited about wanting to live in the same town she grew up in."

"What'd you say?"

"Seward Alaska. Place is wow. But we get to the top and it's beautiful. Fog everywhere, so you can't quite see the mountains but just the tops of some poking through. And I don't know if y'all've been up to Le Conte, but it's this huge rock just sticking out surrounded by small trees. Usually packed but it was just us for a while. So we're eating snacks and I offer her my banana—"

"Woah!" said Chuck, "On a first date?"

"No. Like…nice. So we're eating, talking, starting to go deep. She tells me her story, I tell her mine. Then we start talking about relationships—"

"Did you tell her you've never dated?"

"Yeah. But we're talking and she asks me if I believe in soulmates."

"Do you?"

"Gosh no. But I said yes. That led to me asking what her ideal guy was—"

"Me obviously."

"Ha. But she says Christian, funny, smart, can laugh at themselves, adventurous like finding Atlantis or Womack's treasure, caring. And she's saying all this and in my head I'm thinking she's describing me. And she gets to the end and she says how hard it is to find guys like that. And in my infinite wisdom," he took a deep breath knowing full well the coming reaction, "I look at her and say, 'Sometimes what you're looking for is right in front of you.'"

A collective groan echoed throughout the house. A pillow hit Gilbert in the face.

"You did not say that."

"Gil, no."

"Not gonna lie, pretty smooth."

"I know. Not proud of it. Funny thing though, right after I said it I had to look away to keep from laughing."

"Ah that's so cringe. What'd she say?"

"She smiled and asked me the same question, so I said my ideal guy would probably be me. She laughed, but I wanted to be honest so I just described my ideal girl."

"Young. On your team."

"Into stars and all that."

"That was one time. No. Adventurous, curious, ambitious, doesn't need me to always entertain. A bit of a screw loose. Christian. So that happens and we start going back down—"

"Wait. Back up. What did she say?"

"She said okay, but it was a happy okay, I think." His phone buzzed again. "But that happens and we start back down. And we're talking, laughing. We drive back and it's all good. She did mention how she'd probably never date anyone on her team, but she knows I'm switching schools so I'm thinking that's what she's implying." Gilbert noticed Ezekiel and Chuck share a glance. "Dropped her off around four and asked if she'd be interested in doing something again."

"And?"

"She said probably."

"Let's freaking go."

"Good stuff," said Ezekiel, "Sounds like a really fun time. Has she texted you yet?"

"I reached out last night saying thanks and how fun it was, but she was going to a party so that's probably why I haven't heard anything. Any ideas for a second date?"

The rest of the morning was spent watching soccer and debating nonsensical topics. Around eleven-thirty Gilbert excused himself and drove home.

The next few weeks would be hell. At work two projects were going out that required another run through of drawings and calculations. Monday night he was giving a talk for ministry. Tuesday night he was leading a bible study for high schoolers. Wednesday was his own. Thursday he planned to call John to see how the move to France went. At some point he needed to drive back to Chattanooga to see his parents. Had it really been a month? No. Two months? Gilbert's favorite song came over the radio, drowning another call.

The stench of week-old trash smacked Gilbert in the face as he walked into his apartment. He cracked a window then fell on his couch for a nap. Two hours later he woke to three missed calls from his siblings and a message from Rebecca. His heart grew.

'hey! Yeah yesterday was fun lol but to be completely honest-'

His heart shriveled.

'-I think right now I'm called to just focus on myself! Sorry haha'

Gilbert squeezed the phone. Yesterday was fun? Called to focus on myself? He fell back. What did he do wrong? He replayed the date in his head, kicking himself at every little mistake. He should've never pushed to do the whole trail. What was he thinking showing her the book? Asking about her ideal guy? His stomach convulsed.

'Hey! Sorry to hear that.' No. That sounded bad. *'Hey! No problem.'* Nope. *'Hey! All's good! Completely—'* She already used 'completely'. *'Hey! All's good! Totally understand! Think that's awesome! If you change your mind just let me know!'* He hit send and tossed the phone across the couch.

Should he tell Ezekiel? No, he was with Alex. Chuck? Hooper? Gilbert wallowed in self-pity. Again, he tried to figure out the problem. Maybe it was him. Maybe he was not enough. Gilbert knew he was overthinking, but after twenty-three years of singleness the question lurked in the recesses of his mind.

He had an idea. Grabbing his phone and a box of mint cookies, he began to research Atlantis. Layla London, the great treasure hunter, chemist, doctor — everything really — already found it. Gilbert frowned. He followed her religiously, how did he miss it?

Womack's treasure? Now that was a different story. Layla started looking but gave up. If he could find her, maybe she would help? Maybe she had notes or papers. He dug deeper. She was last seen in Colombia. Flights were cheap. He could leave that day.

Gilbert felt the rush of excitement. He was going on an adventure! To hell with anything else. Work would manage. Ministry would be there when he got back. He'd have stories to tell. People would be wowed.

He raced to his closet and ripped through piles of boxes for a suitable bag. Nothing too big. Nothing too flashy. He needed functional, discrete. He grabbed a dull-gray leather pack.

Clothes? They sold socks and underwear in South America, right? Of course they did. Bring only the essentials. An extra pair of pants. A couple shirts. Toothbrush. Comb. He went back and forth from room to room, forming and reforming the list in his mind, tightly rolling and unrolling, stuffing and unstuffing.

What else? Charger. Camera. That should do it. He looked around one last time. Next stop, Colombia.

Again the phone started to buzz. Gilbert stared at his brother's name on the screen. The walls of his apartment started to fall away, and a bitter cold ate at his skin.

"Gilbert," said John, "you may want to get that. Might be important."

"No. I'd rather not."

"Why?"

Gilbert smiled weakly and turned to say a joke but found no one. He was alone on top of a rock in the middle of a frozen field talking to himself.

Home. There was no home. Not anymore.

The storm had calmed. In the distance he saw a trail of smoke and a dark figure.

37 ... The Town of Brockton

What remained of the empty gray buildings sneered at Gilbert.

Nearly every roof was collapsed under centuries of snow, and years of the seasonal frost-thaw-frost-thaw had eaten away whole walls. He jumped when something scurried past.

"You're good. You're good." He continued searching.

Shattered plates. Scattered boxes. Upturned furniture. Scenes of an unwillingly abandoned town. Was it always like this, or had others found it? No bodies or signs of a fight, but weather and animals could hide that. He came to the final door. He pushed, but something blocked the way. Come on. He threw his shoulder into it. The door budged an inch. Again.

Behind him was a loud thump.

"Hello?"

Gilbert waited. More hallucinations. He returned to the door. With another push it swung in, knocking down a wall of debris. The room was small, filled with a sleeping bag and scraps of food. The orange embers of a dying fire glowed in an old stone chimney.

He shouted Angela's name.

No reply.

Removing his pack he stretched, letting the tired muscles breathe. He'd feel awful in the morning. Oh well.

A tired chest tucked into the corner caught his eye. Pulling it out, he found stacks of letters.

May 3, 1623

I have found paradise! The days are endless. Food is abundant. Westfal returned with a beast larger than any I have ever seen! The water is cool and good. Most of all, we are far from those who hunt us. The Spanish captain will never find us here. The men's families are due to arrive any day. The extra hands will make building much easier. - D.W.

May 12, 1623

My family has arrived! Lily has never looked more beautiful. Charles has grown so much — he will certainly be a strong one.

And hopefully smarter. The town is coming together quickly and smiles are on every face. Some of the woman complain about the sun never going below. Who cares?! Is not heaven to be like this? - D.W.

May 28, 1623

Westfal reports seeing figures on the horizon. Could they be the Spanish??? Unlikely. I have ordered him to keep quiet. No reason to panic the town. - D.W.

Jun 3, 1623

THEY ARE NOT THE SPANISH!!!

What the women call 'savages' arrived this morning with gifts. I have traveled far and long enough to know these are native tribesmen, same as I am from England. 'Savages', what nonsense. We offered in return what we could; no reason to make enemies. They do not seem eager to involve themselves with us, nor I them. Also, the moon briefly appeared. - D.W.

July 17, 1623

Westfal reports seeing packs of dogs on the horizon. Crockett also mentioned tracks not far from town. Wild, dangerous animals. I have ordered everyone to be careful. This is not the city. On a better note, Lily and I have been trying to have another

child. A daughter, perhaps. I might name her after my mother.
Charles is excited for his first hunt. He has made a game of
'sneaking' on me as I work and attacking with a spoon. Life is
good. Retiring was the right choice. - D.W.

August 23, 1623
The first snow has fallen early. Is that common for these
parts? The children race around laughing and playing. I have
ordered the men to prepare extra wood and meat. Just in case.
The days are still long but getting shorter. - D.W.

August 29, 1623
LILY IS PREGNANT!!!!!
We were watching the sky lights when she told me. She thinks
it is a daughter. - D.W.

September 1, 1623
The Yukotta tribe, as they call themselves, surprised us today
with another visit and more gifts: thick, thick, thick coats made of
white fur. Imagine the size of the creatures! Very kind gesture,
one we graciously repaid with a meal, but a gesture not needed.
It is far too warm for such attire. Maybe their kind chills easily?
- D.W.

September 15, 1623

Damn the boy! I told him never to leave town without me or his mother. Westfal and the men managed to kill the dogs, but the damage was already done. Smith says he will have to remove the arm. Possibly the leg. - D.W.

October 2, 1623

The days are much shorter. Charles is walking fine, but he will never be what he could. I blame myself. - D.W.

October 11, 1623

Westfal reports less and less wildlife. Even the lakes are empty. - D.W.

October 17, 1623

Lily is not herself. A darkness has overtaken her. I tell her to take heart, if only for our unborn child. She cried at that. - D.W.

October 20, 1623

Westfal, Cricketts, Long, and myself returned to the Regal today. I miss the open seas. The sun. The thrills. More snow has fallen. - D.W.

October 24, 1623

Charles has fallen ill. I hope for a speedy recovery. - D.W.

October 25, 1623

Charles has died.

October 30, 1623

I buried the boy besides the lake. He always enjoyed fishing there. - D.W.

November 1, 1623

We are short on food. Where are the animals? How do the Yokotta survive? - D.W.

November 5, 1623

The Yokotta's gifts are life saving. - D.W.

November 11, 1623

The Smiths have moved in with the Longs. The house must be used for the fires. - D.W.

November 17, 1623

The McPherson's house collapsed under the snow. Damn the stuff. The rivers are solid as rock. The frost remains even with the fire. Nobody leaves their homes. The sun is hardly seen anymore. Westfal says we need to leave soon before the ship is locked in. I told him to stay strong. We will survive. - D.W.

December 1, 1623

I have doomed these people to a fate worse than death. I promised them Paradise, and instead gave them Hell. We cannot take everyone back. At least not at once. These people are my family. How can I say who leaves and who stays? - D.W.

December 2, 1623

I leave with Westfal and the other men when all are asleep. Forgive me Lily. You deserved better. You all did. I love you.

    - Daniel

A groan from outside snapped Gilbert back. He stuffed the letters into the box and watched the door. Puffs of frozen air shot into the room.

38 ... The Beast

Gilbert pulled out his knife and walked backwards. With each step the shadow grew in detail. It looked like a dog or wolf, but the legs were too long. The ears too round. The neck too large. He held his breath.

Slowly the beast disappeared.

Gilbert exhaled and turned, accidentally knocking over a pile of logs.

Thawk!

Part of the wall exploded and great black jaws snapped through.

He needed an exit. Everywhere he looked was solid wall. The creature's body was beginning to come through the cracks. The house shook from its thunderous roar. He needed out!

Gilbert raced to within reach of the beast and began wildly jabbing his weapon. Thin black blood splattered the walls. The beast wailed. Any moment the wall would completely collapse.

With a great push the beast broke through, and Gilbert rushed out the front door and fell into the snow. Scrambling, he tried to put as much distance between himself and the animal as possible. He would rather freeze than be eaten alive.

His muscles grew tired. Each step was bitter, freezing, soaking wet. His limbs were losing function. He collapsed, exhausted.

The creature let out a low growl.

Life. Death. Who cared what happened to him? He had run. Even if he survived, where would he go? Let it end here. Let the fear, let the guilt, let the loneliness, let it all go away. Tears froze on Gilbert's cheeks. This is what he truly wanted, to go out with a bang.

Just look. Look at the beast. Look how it moves. With power, with hunger, with one thing on its mind. It probably hasn't eaten in weeks. Take out the knife. Use the bag as a shield. No more running. Scream. Shout. Be as large. Be as terrifying. Kick up snow. Howl. Howl! Throw off civilization. If death had come for him, he would fight. He would meet the beast. Don't slow. Don't stop. That's it. Come on! Look at its skin. Its dark, loose, clinging skin. Look how it sags, swinging with each thunderous leap. That sharp, vicious, monstrous face. It shoots smoke like an engine. Its body shakes with each breath. And the eyes. The smooth, black, lifeless eyes with something off about them. Yes. He could see it now. He could see it all. Come on. Come on!

Thirty feet.

Twenty feet.

Fifteen feet.

Ten feet.

Gilbert raised his knife.

Five feet.

Pop!

The beast's head jerked to the side. Blood covered snow. It slowed, wandering aimlessly while struggling to stand.

Gilbert's ear began to ring. His world swirled around. Darkness.

39 ... Survival

Gilbert woke up warm. And naked.

He sat straight and crashed into the rock ceiling.

A bottle shattered nearby.

"Ha! I knew ya'd do that," said Angela. She swayed drunken-ly across the fire, bottle in hand.

As the pain subsided everything came into view. They were in a small cave, the entrance open but barricaded with more boxes and furniture. Along the far wall, close to the fire, hung his wet clothes.

"What happened?"

"I saved ya ass. That's what happened. Angela the bear slayer! No. Not that. Angela the bear killer. Bear barrier? Burier? Ew.

Slicer? Slider? Reckoner? Did I already say slayer? Bear. Bare. Beer."

"Angela."

"What?"

Gilbert closed his eyes and composed himself. "What happened after the avalanche?"

"Oh, that? I found the other key."

"You found the other key?"

"That's what I said. I think. Yeah. After the snow I made for town. And I had a sweet setup in the center until ya came along and brought a damn bear."

"Thought it was you."

"I'm not fat."

"Neither was the bear."

"Compared ta a bear I'm not!"

Focus. "Were you looking for me?"

"Of course! Ya have the other key."

"And if I didn't?"

She waved him off. "Called in a few favors. Storm is keeping our ride from reaching us so may be a day or two. Anything else ya need ta know? Oh, want ta see the full gibber?" She snapped the two keys together and shined her light.

EEHEEOEPCESTIWALISACIEOE

NIWSVTLEAHIRRAERTNHELHDR

EMDTKENSUNROTEYEFYSDEBOE

AFOORANLNWWWEUITBUMANOAT

WYFYDMESROOTHRLTEOTSATPR

BDNAEMASTKCNHCABIFINLMTVE

RRRUODDEBTNOPNVEUIYRCTNH

"Can't make anything of it. Oh, help ya'self ta some drinks. Found all this wine stored away. And the bear meat should hold us over."

"Why am I naked?"

"Cause ya clothes were wet and we only have one sleeping bag and I don't want ta freeze. Which reminds me." Angela began to undress and hang up her own clothes. "Scooch."

Gilbert's soul left his body. "I'm not sure if I'm, well, if I'm comfortable with this."

"Get over it. If — 'scuse me — if I recall, this was ya idea. 'Ya got ta share the warmth Angela,' or something like that. Well, prepare for the warmth ta be shared."

As she slid next to him he tried to focus on anything else. How many chips were in the ceiling? One. Two. Three…

"Ya gonna have ta adjust."

"I'm good."

"I'm not spending the whole night with the back of ya hands on my ass."

"Well where do you want them?"

The next few minutes were spent awkwardly adjusting and readjusting from one position to the next. Angela finally grabbed Gilbert's hand and pressed it into her stomach.

"And that's what a normal person does. Sometimes ya so weird, ya know?"

Seventy. Seventy-one. Seventy-two. Seventy-three. Wait, that one's already been counted. One. Two. Three…

"Oh no," said Angela.

"What?"

"I'm suddenly pregnant."

"Shut up."

Angela arched her neck so they looked at the other. He could smell the alcohol on her breath.

"I don't get ya Gil. I mean, ya pressed up against the most beautiful woman in the world—"

"Bit of a stretch." His side erupted in pain.

"—in the world. And ya clam up like a clam. What gives?"

"Just trying to be respectful."

"Well, with all due respect, that's the biggest load of bull I've ever heard. If I had ta guess, I'd say ya never done it before."

"I haven't."

Angela pulled away. "Really? Hold on. Are ya one of those 'wait-till-marriage' freaks? And what about the Queen?"

"Not counting that. And no. Maybe." How to word this? Gilbert answered honestly. "It plays into it. But I haven't been in the situation where I want to. It hasn't felt right. I don't want to force it or just do it to do it. Seems cheap. Back home I also do high school ministry. Couldn't tell a kid he shouldn't be doing it if I am."

"And if a kid does, ya kick him ta the curb?"

"No. Never. I always tell the guys that no matter what they do I'll still be there for them."

"Sure ya will."

"I've been in there shoes. It's a weird time."

Angela started to laugh. "I'm trying ta picture teenage Gilbert."

"Braces. Buzz cut. Wore the same green tie with silver shamrocks all four years. Busted up hiking shoes — same pair as my dad. What else? Zero confidence, and an obsession with getting a girlfriend." He smiled at the thought of the foolish, awkward kid. "What about you?"

"Ponytail. Jumpsuit. Revolver. I wanted ta try soccer but Mama thought team sports were a waste of time. Made me do dance instead. Hated it."

"I went out for football my sophomore year. Weighed one-hundred pounds soaking wet. Had absolutely no business being out there but I wanted to stick it to my dad. First practice, first drill, got knocked five yards through the air."

"And thus ended the athletic career of Gilbert Casanova."

"Hell no!" he laughed. "Fell in love with it. Put everything I had into getting better. Never really played in games, and knew I probably wouldn't, but I had a role and I enjoyed it. Work hard, give a good look in practice, lead by example."

"Ya dad must've been so proud," she snorted. "What about all those horrible stories ya talked about?"

Gilbert shifted his arm. "There was this time when I was seven, maybe eight, and I couldn't fall asleep. So I go to my parent's room and started knocking on the door. My dad calls out, tells me to go back to bed. So I walk back to my room. Still can't sleep. I go again. Same thing. And again—"

"What color pajamas did ya wear?"

"—and after the fourth time I go back my dad about rips the door out. Mom's screaming and crying. Brothers and sister are poking their heads out from their rooms. Dad's yelling and swearing. And he starts dragging me down the stairs. And there I am, holding on to the banister for dear life. Well, eventually he pulls my fingers free and tosses me outside. Lights go out and people go to sleep."

"Mine were blue. With little camels on 'em. My favorite animal was a camel, ya know. I had one of those stuffed toys."

"Next night we're all eating dinner together laughing about it." Gilbert smiled weakly. "He was always tough, especially on himself, but he did the best he could. And I was by no means perfect. I added a lot of pain, a lot of stress. The older I get the more I realize everyone is just doing what they think is right and hoping it works out. Sometimes it does. Sometimes it doesn't. No one's perfect."

Angela rolled around, a confused look on her face. "That's it? I thought ya said it was a horror story? Horr-or. That's just parenting. Nothing horrible happened. Ya just didn't listen. No wonder ya family hates ya."

"Thanks."

"Oh don't get all mopey on me."

"Fine. What do you think is horrible?"

Angela cracked her neck. "For starters? Oh, sending ya daughter inta' the rainforests."

"That's not bad. Seems kind of fu…" Gilbert stared at her. Angela's hair was a disheveled mess. Her face was tired and dirty. Nostrils flared. The corner of her mouth twitched. Veined eyes helplessly looked to him.

"Ya know, funny thing Gilby." She moved so she was on her back. "It wasn't until after the Amazon that it…that it… Before we'd sit around and brag about missions. Sing songs. Laugh. It

238

was fun. I was fine. Then they went and threw me out. My friends. My family."

"Angela I—"

"I still hear the flamethrowers, ya know. Just this big whoosh and roar." She tried to imitate the noise. "I still hear the cries of families running from us. The smells. Ash everywhere. We made a few snow angels. Well, ash angels, I guess. We were supposed ta be the good guys, ya know. We were after this statue. Marble, purple jewels. Real pretty. It was supposed ta be easy. The grand arrival of Madame Silver's protege. The one, the only, duh duh dah — Jericho Silver."

She looked away. "Gilby, we were there for nine months. Nine. It was supposed ta be a week. On the first day we crossed a river. Piranhas. Lost two. Next something happened with our food. That's another four. Jeremiah got crushed by a snake. Oh, and then half of us got captured by cannibals. Do ya know what it's like ta live in a cage for three months? Ta force ya'self ta eat people? Ya own people?"

"They all looked up ta me. And I watched 'em get dragged off. I tried ta fight. I really tried." Her hands moved towards her head. "I still hear 'em. I can't get 'em out. They keep asking why I failed. They keep saying it should've been me. It should've been me, Gilbert."

"I hid in the back. They kept coming for us so I hid. Every time I'd just black out and hope ta never wake up. One night they forgot ta lock the door, so I killed 'em all. I thought I would feel good, but I didn't. I felt horrible. And then after all that, after ya lose everyone around ya, ya finally find the damn statue. And guess what? It's broken. Just a pile of dust and stones and piss. It was disgraceful. Jericho had no right ta come back. She knew it. So I left her there. And the worst part is, she never wanted ta go in the first place. She knew she wasn't ready. We all did." A bitter smile flashed. "But Mama knows best, ya know. And I thought she'd understand. Whenever she messed up I understood. Instead I lose everything. My home. My family. My life. I just want things ta go back ta normal. How they used ta be, ya know."

Gilbert stared at the frost. "Yeah."

Outside the sky lit up and the snow showed like a field of diamonds. Tails of color — greens to blues to purples to reds — silently raced through the night. They circled, cut, jumped, skipped, and skopped in every wild direction. Gilbert had never seen something so beautiful.

He felt Angela lean into him, stretching her neck for a better view.

Part 7
France

December 28, 2021

40 ... Paris

Gilbert leaned his head against a wall and closed his eyes. What an idiot. He really couldn't get anything right.

A light rain fell over Orly airport. People poured from the building in steady intervals, their purposes easy enough to guess. The parents struggling to control children running and screaming in circles were probably here after thinking Paris was a suitable group destination. The young men in cheap suits talking loudly on phones were most likely low-level accountants or lawyers trying to show off. Young tourists new to travel sat sulking in loose sweatpants and open-toed shoes, dissatisfied that the City of Romance was a dull gray rather than the pinks and yellows of their dreams. Armed officers chatted under covered areas. Gilbert wondered if they could tell what he was there for. Surely he looked like any other witless foreigner.

Pulling his cap low and scarf tighter he resumed searching his bag.

Seven days during recovery were spent meticulously planning every detail and accounting for whatever obstacle was thrown their way. They were to arrive separately and meet at a hostel named *Le serpent d'émeraude*. Early in the morning a train would take them to Bordeaux, then Bordeaux to Brive where John would be ready with two horses and whatever supplies they'd requested. With any luck they'd find the treasure within three days. He might even have time to sightsee.

Angela did warn him to be on guard. Strangers, rival hunters, scammers — specifically those of the La'Vidi family — could be waiting for them. After the incident in America, it was all but guaranteed.

Of course, all this hinged on Gilbert actually making it to the city, a critical but overlooked step.

His first priority was getting his phone to work. He tried inserting a paper clip. Too big. A wire. A key. People shot glances as they walked by. He reached all the way to the bottom and pulled out a watch that he'd haphazardly thrown in — a style statement that was now his last hope.

With animalistic fervor he tore the device to pieces. He held the thin shaft between two fingers. Please work. The compartment clicked. Yes! Gilbert clenched his fist in pride. Minutes later he was connected.

Now how did he get to the city? Train? taxi? What did taxis look like in Europe? A line of black SUVs were parked nearby. Swallowing, he approached and tapped on the window.

"Hello. Bonjour. Taxi?" he said. The snakes tattooed on the driver's hands stretched in annoyance. "Passe vous English?"

The man broke into rapid French and threw his arms in wild animation. Gilbert would find no help.

He walked to an officer in a bright orange vest, and again he was met with the same confused look.

"Passe? Vous? English?" The officer repeated.

Was he saying it wrong?

A feeling of hopelessness began to set. He survived death, torture, criminal negations, a volcano, and a whole host of other thrills. But this, a simple language barrier, was going to be his end.

A gloved hand grabbed his shoulder.

41 ... Marco

"Pardon! Pardon!" The man was older, light sags under the eyes, and bald save for the patch of gray encircling his skull. His dark pants matched a pullover with the silver letters 'L-V' embroidered on the right breast. "Bonjour! Quel est le problème?"

The officer stepped forward. "Je ne sais pas. Occupez-vous de cet étranger."

The man turned to Gilbert. "Get in. I take you." Before he could process what was happening, the man pushed Gilbert into a van and slammed the door. He tried to open it. Locked.

The man started the car. "My name Marco. Where you go?"

He thought fast. Best to play dumb. Gilbert fumbled with his phone and showed a restaurant a few streets from the hostel.

"How much this gonna be? Don't wanna be screwed or anything."

Marco's laugh seemed forced. "Ah, first time? So set rate airport to city. Before river is thirty. After river is thirty-five. I take you. No worry. Where you from?" They took off.

"Tennessee. United States."

"Ah! United States! All the protests and racists! Would not want to be black man or I would get shot, no?"

What was happening? Gilbert remained silent.

"I been to New York City. My cousin live there. Dirty place. Pigeons. Nasty rats. Fun if younger. Now where Tennessee? North? South?"

"South. A little above Florida."

"Florida! Crazy people live in Florida. Disney World there, though. Tennessee like Florida?"

"Gosh I hope not."

Marco didn't laugh.

Gilbert continued. "Do you know Knoxville? Memphis? Nashville?"

"Nashville! All the music. Elvis Presley. Johnny Cash. Maybe one day I go."

Gilbert let the conversation die off. He watched the passing outskirts. Reds and blues and greens and yellows were painted on rusted supports. Lone weeds grew out of cracks. Litter rested against barriers. The air seemed heavier, grittier.

His stomach cried. With sad realization the last meal he ate was a soggy cheese sandwich twelve hours and a flight earlier, and the last sip of water before. The effects of travel were starting to weigh on him. A warm meal and rest would set him right.

"Marco, any recommendations on where to eat?"

"To eat? You hungry? Here," Marco tossed a handful of packages that looked like off-brand Twinkies. "I show few spots before drop off. Everywhere food good. Everywhere. You go stall? Good. You go store? Good. My favorite, turkey leg wrapped in bacon. Very very good. My wife, she do not agree." Marco pointed out the various locations.

They pulled to the side. "Alright. See green sign," he motioned to a flashing cross above a corner store called *Nourriture pas chère*. "Best food in France. I let you go. Since south it will be thirty."

As the machine read his card, Gilbert checked for anything missing. "Well, I appreciate the ride and tips. Have a great day Marco."

"Yes yes. Welcome to my city." Before he reached the curb the car was gone.

Gilbert rounded the corner and took a seat and exhaled. So, this was Paris.

Old men smiled, talking, tossing crumbs to gray pigeons. Parents swung kids. Groups of students stared into shops. Smells of baked honey floated out windows. He'd sacrifice another finger — a whole hand, even — for a croissant.

He took out his phone and checked his location. If he had more energy he'd probably be livid, but all he could offer was a weak sigh. He was eight miles south of his destination.

42 ... A Long Day

Gilbert started walking.

It was a beautiful city. Not too loud. Not too busy. All the buildings looked like they belonged in a museum.

Emerging from the alleys, Gilbert assumed the massive structure to his right was for government. It reminded him of his own capitol building, only larger. Thousands of well-dressed individuals went about their day, stopping only to look as he took pictures. Later he happened across the great Notre Dame cathedral where hundreds of tourists gawked and peddlers tried to sell goods. The place was impressive, but part of him expected more. As he neared his destination, Gilbert passed a growing protest.

Weaving through the crowd, he noticed police cars slowly edging in and officers forming a circle.

He made a note to look into the laws of the country.

Finally he saw the hostel. The illuminated sign stood right on the corner. His stomach painfully called out again. Angela could wait. Food first. A quiet looking door called his name. Answering, he found himself in an empty Mediterranean restaurant. After a series of hand motions and head shakes and various smiles with the Arabic waiter, a feast of rice, chicken, and vegetables found its way in front of him.

Gilbert sat eating in peaceful silence. He could feel strength returning to his limbs. For the moment life was good. His phone buzzed.

"Where the hell are ya?"

Within minutes the door swung open. Angela looked the same as when they first met, although slightly cleaner. And calmer. She seemed less guarded. A smile stretched from ear to ear. "Fancy seeing ya. Come here often?" She took a seat and tore into his rice. Bits of food flew as she talked.

"Ya know, I thought the plan was ta meet at the hostel. But oh no! The great Gilfanso Casanobody thinks he's too good for Angela Bronte. Leaves her sitting at the bar ta fend for herself. Ya know, some guy, real slimy type — gosh this food is good — slicked hair, bulging arms, zero legs, unbuttoned shirt. The whole shebang. Dude walks in on a cloudy day wearing sunglasses and doesn't take 'em off. I mean," she rolled her head, "come on. It's dark as hell inside bud. But anyways, this guy saunters on over, trying ta look all cool, and challenges me ta a drinking contest. Says if he wins, he gets ta take me out. I play along, and so I meekly say, 'And what if I win?' — dude laughs and says I can do whatever I want. Long story short," she cracked her knuckles and sat back proudly, "he left with a broken nose."

"Ever consider a job in foreign relations?"

She raised an eyebrow. "Run inta' any problems?"

He told her of his adventure.

"Eh. I think we're good," she said. "The Vids would've made themselves known. Probably some fashion statement."

Following dinner they retired to their room. The single bed took up half the space, along with two desks shoved against the far walls. Dual windows reached floor to ceiling and looked out across the green roofs and darkening skies of Paris. Squinting, he could make out the pointed top of the Eiffel Tower. If his life didn't hang in the balance, it would've been nice. He closed the bedside curtains and changed.

"You bring a charger? Phones almost out."

"Yeah," Angela called from the bathroom. "Middle pocket. Ya need ta use the converter or it'll fry."

Why did Europe use different amps? Or was it volts? Gilbert searched for an outlet closer to the bed, but the only one was beneath a table at the other end. After making sure the device actually charged, he laid it on the table and turned to the window.

Any creep could look straight in. Best to close those too.

"Don't turn around." The excitement in Angela's voice made him nervous. He heard the bed squeak. A million different scenarios rushed through his head. "I said don't turn. Close ya eyes. Alright," she yawned. "Voila."

Gilbert let go of the curtain.

"J'ai l'air d'un stupide garçon américain, n'est-ce pas?" Angela Bronte excitedly bobbed up and down on the mattress.

"Je French is mucho badio."

She threw her feet out and fell back. "I said I look like a stupid American boy."

Now he noticed the yellow beanie.

"I'm honored." He joined her. Gosh was he tired.

"That's it? That's all ya got for me?"

"It's good fashion?"

Her jaw flexed. "Last time I try ta be nice."

Oh, come on. "What do you want me to do? I- I think it's awesome. Really brings out your eyes?"

"Ya reaching. Saw it and thought it'd be funny, ya know. Is it that hard ta imagine?"

Yes, but Gilbert kept that to himself. "I really do appreciate it. You look almost as good as me."

The phone buzzed on the desk, saving him. "Probably John. Was supposed to call tonight." He rolled off the bed.

What an odd turn of events. Was she actually warming up to him?

"Stop!"

Gilbert froze.

"A foot above the desk. In line with ya phone."

The shaking red dot was nearly invisible.

43 ... A Very Long Day

"Bonsoir! Pouvez-vous envoyer des draps supplémentaires dans la chambre cinq-zéro-deux, s'il vous plaît? Merci." Angela put down the service phone.

Gilbert finished tying his shoes and shouldered his bag. "That the police?"

"Not exactly. I'd say we got two, maybe three minutes."

"Until?"

Angela continued stuffing her bag. "I got a couple tickets ta Nice. Gare Montparnasse. Train leaves in an hour."

"Two minutes to what?

"Do exactly as I do. Don't think. Don't stop. Just go. Ya got that? I wanna hear ya say it."

He repeated her commands. What was happening? His vision narrowed. His hands shook. Gilbert tried to quiet his mind, but the more he focused the louder the world became.

The shudder and shakes of hidden pipes behind walls. The abrupt start-stop of a buzzing fly. The irregular creaks from uneven boards. The steady hum of an electric fan. Tired groans when he shifted on the mattress. A door slamming. The phone vibrating. His heart pounding. Angela breathing. That tick-tick-ticking. Damn! He'd never heard such an infernal sound!

Gilbert instinctively grabbed his wrist then remembered his watch was gone.

There was a knock at the door. "Service d'étage! Room service!"

The pieces started to fit. He looked at Angela. "Please no."

Her shoulders tightened. "We're going through that window. Entrez!"

As the bullet ripped through one window, Gilbert and Angela crashed through the other. Shards of glass tore his clothes and skin. He rolled awkwardly, tables and chairs and whatever else snapping like twigs and causing a great deal of commotion.

He struggled to his feet.

Pop!

Bits of stone exploded.

The gap was widening. Angela vaulted roof to roof, railing to railing.

Come one! Move!

"The door won't open!"

He rammed with his shoulder. Bodies and wood scattered.

Ping! A bottle burst.

Crash! Another disintegrated against his arm.

A woman shrieked under covers while a bare-chested man scrambled for another weapon. What were they doing? He wasn't the killer. Don't waste them on him!

A large figure in black filled the balcony. Gilbert rolled, slipping twice on the squandered vintage before reaching the stairs. The screams behind him climbed in desperation then abruptly stopped.

Doors flew open. Curious residents peered out. Who was this madman interrupting dinner? And on a Monday, no less?

Metal whizzed past and cut a hole in the blue wall right behind his throat. Gilbert launched himself down a level and smashed into the weak plaster.

Zip! Shots were getting closer.

Keep going! Nearly there!

In the brief second between exiting the building and reaching Angela, his eye caught a thin reflective line silently flowing from the ear of a crumpled body at the base of a moped. Without a word he joined her and they tore away in a cloud of dirt and rubber.

Breathe. Focus. Breathe. Just move on. Don't think about it. Everyone is probably fine.

"Hey!" Angela's skull crashed into his nose. "I said quit squeezing so damn tight. Look up directions ta get ta the station."

"Left my phone."

"Use mine. Code is one-one-one-one-one-one."

The streets blurred together in a cocktail of exhaust fumes and adrenaline. Overhead, blue snowflakes and green trees and red spiral candies lit the road. Hobbling beggars mingled with the stumbling partiers coming out into the night, oblivious to the deadly game of cat and mouse taking place. When they arrived at the station they ditched the vehicle and headed straight for the platforms. Within minutes the machine lurched forward.

His body refused to remain still. How could it? Gilbert stretched his wine-soaked legs in the otherwise empty car. He wanted to jump. To fight! The electrifying tunnel of animalistic desire was still rolling, but it was only a matter of time before he devolved into a mess of sleep deprived movements and incomplete sentences. Was it even safe to sleep? Maybe they could take shifts. He collapsed into the seat across from Angela intending to suggest his plan.

As he prepared the words his tongue diverted. "Did you know all that would happen?"

Angela stared out beyond the glass and passing shadows. "Gonna need ya ta be a 'lil more 'pacific, Gilbo." Her eyes briefly fell then widened.

"Did you know about the maid? The couple? What about the bike you took?"

"The maid, yeah. Used it once in Beijing. And Cairo. And Moscow. Actually, funny story. I used it on the fella who taught me. The couple? I'm guessing by the way ya asking they dipped? Nah. That wasn't planned but it 'twas possible." Angela's face narrowed and she bit her lower lip in thought. "It's probably nothing, but I've neva heard of the La'Vidis just killing civilians. Or attacking out in the open. Usually talk first, want a slice of the pie type. I don't like it."

"What you thinking?"

"I…I don't know."

Gilbert searched his memories. Marco? Father Don? Caroline? Caroline! Who else could know their plans? "Angela, I wasn't totally honest about the queen. She threatened to tell people we were looking for the key if I didn't do exactly what she said."

Angela's head fell. "God damnit Gilbert." She muttered her Spanish. "Why didn't ya tell me?"

261

The feeling of powerlessness slowly crept through his body. "I wanted to forget the whole thing."

"Quit being a baby."

Go to hell.

Besides the low rumble of the speeding vehicle, all was silent. "What now? We catch a train from Nice? Sleep on the ride down?"

"Nah. We'll get off at one of the stops, catch a train from there. Can't have people following us, ya know. Should be about three hours." She let loose an emphatic yawn.

"I'll take first watch. Wake you in an hour or so."

"Ya gonna change?"

"Before we get off. Get some rest."

Angela wedged her bag in a corner and was snoring in seconds.

He settled in and bravely fended off the sweet invader for nearly thirty minutes before finally succumbing to his wounds. It was a valiant effort by all accounts. Two-and-a-half hours later he was awakened by the conductor.

"Billet, s'il vous plaît."

Gilbert fumbled for the phone.

"Merci." The man continued to the next car.

Gilbert gently prodded Angela until a semi-coherent sound answered. There was something ironic about a person like her sleeping so heavily.

"We're getting off in thirty. I'm gonna go change."

She lifted her elbow and let it drop.

Taking the last set of clean clothes from his bag, he made for the bathroom. Gilbert carefully peeled back the ribboned layers and frowned at the many cuts and bruises he'd accumulated. Hopefully John still kept extra supplies on hand. Next he slid on the dry set. Not knowing when his next chance would be, Gilbert sat and emptied.

The door shook.

"Occupied." He returned to his thoughts. They'd probably have to walk to John's unless he could remember the number. What was it? 754? 756? 745? Again someone pulled. Gilbert knocked and repeated himself. Was there no privacy for the weary? Surely there was another bathroom at the other end. The pulling continued. "Alright, give me a second." He finished and stuffed the damp clothes into a plastic bag. It was probably an old man, hard-hearing, minimal regard for others. Gilbert put on a smile and unlocked the door.

A gloved hand wrenched it open and went straight for Gilbert's throat.

44 ... A Very, Very Long Day

The wire coiled around Gilbert's neck. He fell back against the seat and kicked wildly.

The dark figure took up the entire room. Hot, rancid breaths rushed from behind a black mask.

His vision flickered. Air. He needed air! With a well-placed kick the attacker stumbled into the door, giving Gilbert just enough time to slip three fingers between the loose wires and escape the trap.

He looked for the lock. Where was Angela? Where was his knife? A knee shot into his stomach.

In darkness they wrestled. Limbs and skulls clanged off metal. The mirror shattered. Incoherent gasps and gurgles and grunts mixed with short cries of exertion. If he could just get around. Signal for help. Something. Anything!

A fist cracked against Gilbert's jaw. He collapsed, dazed. He had no energy left. A thick hand seized him by the hair and rammed his face into the slimy abyss. The stench of piss and shit clogged his throat. Tiny specks latched onto his lips. He was choking on the fumes!

Breathe. Brea— Breathe. Breathe! Not like this. Not like this. Something close to the sound of a caged animal rattled from his mouth. He could feel his mind slipping.

Gilbert summoned what strength he could and pushed. Everything now! His back and shoulders screamed. Push!

At the breaking point he stopped fighting and let his chest crash. As hoped, the sudden change was enough to stagger his opponent. He surfaced. Bile filled his mouth. Gilbert dodged a strike. Again he kicked.

A slick hand found him and squeezed. He clawed, ripping latex and cloth and skin. The blue gloves turned purple. Tattoos of snakes lined the attacker's arm. They showed no emotion, no struggle, no anything.

Gilbert's fingers looked for anything within reach. Out of all the ways to go, the bathroom of a French train? The toilet! He snagged the dripping plastic and swung.

His opponent fell.

He stood over the body, his heart trying to escape his chest. Something inside him stirred. Something…something continued to fight. To work the flames licking his blood. His hand tightened around the cold plastic.

Give in.

Leave, it's over.

They'll only come back.

Stop. Focus. Breathe.

Take it. Take the advantage!

Stop it.

They'll come for everyone.

Get out.

They'll kill everyone.

Get out.

Weak. Failure. Coward!

Get out!

His mind went empty except for the simple goal of survival and the smell of mint and the awful buzz. It was like watching someone else control his body.

The figure raised its hands. The seat disintegrated, splintering, shrapnel flying in every direction. The arms fell. Still Gilbert swung until all that remained was a fist sized chunk of warm plastic and an unsatisfied thirst an a pool of blood.

45 ... A Very, Very, Very Long Day

Air shot out of Gilbert's nose in violent bursts. He kicked the lifeless body fully expecting it to lunge. The corpse fell to its side, motionless.

The fog cleared. What did he do? What did he just do? He dropped the weapon and tried to move. This was all a dream. He reached for support and found none. Please no. He landed with a thud against the broken toilet. Please no.

"Get up. Get up. F- Fight me. Come on, get up."

It stared back at him. A single, unwavering, blue eye.

He did what was needed. H- He had no choice. It was life or death. It was self-defense, not murder.

The tears were like acid.

Focus. Breathe. There's still a job. Move on. Move on. Move on.

There was a heavy knock.

"Ya fall in? We're about ta get off."

He struggled to his feet and opened the door.

Angela looked at him then the body. Her face grew pale.

"We're leaving."

They stepped off the train onto a simple concrete platform. Intermittent lighting illuminated the way through a sleepy town that decided stopped modernizing at some point in the late 1800's.

He rubbed his arms. Damn the cold. "Where are we?"

Angela spun around a few times, "I think Brive? Breve? Bread? Whatever that sign says."

"Why?"

"There's a station on the other side of town that can take us ta ya friend. We got off here ta buy a lil time. I told ya this, ya know."

"How far?"

"Five miles. Bridge at the half-way point. Are ya gonna talk or keep acting like a child?"

He pushed past.

Damn this town. Damn this trip. Damn everything! It had to be a dream. It- It had to be. A really, really, really bad, awful dream. Gilbert flinched when a black SUV sped by on the highway to his right. Who would be out driving this late? Why are there so many gas stations? Where did the houses go?

His heart felt ready to explode. Please. He had to get away from the train. Put it in the past. Move away. Move on.

Asphalt turned to iron as he reached the bridge. A cold wind blew up from the black river below.

"Gilbert."

"What!" He wheeled around. "What do you want? Want me to blow up an- an orphanage? Cr- Crash a plane? Rob a bank?"

"I want ya ta act normal."

He started to laugh.

"Normal? Normal? What does that even mean? N- Nothing about this is normal. We were just chased through Paris. We were shot at. Shot. At. I can't even go to the bathroom without someone trying to kill me. Normal? Nothing about any of this — any of this — is normal!"

"Grow up."

Gilbert's vision phased in and out.

"You can't talk. You, going on and on and on about 'Mama'. Mama wants this. Mama wants that. Mama will be so happy to have me back. Damnit Angela! When will you see she doesn't care about you! Look at your back. Look at your life. She's tried to kill you. When will you get it through your thick, stupid, stubborn skull?"

Without a word Angela dropped her bag and jumped into the river.

And Gilbert laughed. Not intentionally, but instinctively. Like breathing.

It started slow. A cough. Gradually it grew. He'd been beaten, bloodied, betrayed, bruised, raped, shot, killed a man, let an island burn, run from his family, and watched the people he loved die. He found the treasure he so desperately craved, and it brought nothing.

His stomach hurt from laughter and tears streamed down his face. He kept laughing and rolling, the cries echoing through the otherwise silent valley. He kept laughing, even as his vision began to phase in and out. He kept laughing, even as the laughs grew weaker and weaker until Gilbert Casanova finally laid sobbing and gasping for breath in the red snow.

55 ... The Mind of a Killer

Gilbert didn't know how long he was out. He remembered flashes. Swinging lights, masked faces, the smell of cigarettes. Whenever he tried to move, some unseen force held him in place and eventually he abandoned the fight. How much of his life was a dream? Was he even real? In the sparse moments of consciousness he prayed that if he should wake that he'd find himself back in his bed in Knoxville. He promised he'd change. He'd joke less. He'd take better care of his apartment. He'd do whatever it took for the nightmare to pass into oblivion.

When he finally awoke it took him a moment to adjust to the sunlight pouring into the otherwise dark room. He tried to sit but was still held in place. Restraints on both wrists and ankles.

There was movement to his side and a slender young woman appeared with a device that she shined into his eyes.

"He's stable," she said to someone.

"Thank you. That will be all for now."

The young woman quickly left.

The voice sounded familiar. Gilbert searched but half the room was concealed in shadow.

"You should make a full recovery. My top people are seeing to it."

Silver. He focused his vision and could see her outline in a far corner. He began to fight the restraints. If he could just get free. Just get close enough to wrap a hand around her neck.

"Don't hurt yourself. That isn't chicken wire."

"Where am I? Why am I alive?"

"Where? You are safe. Why? Well, call it making good on a deal." She came into the light and was hardly recognizable. She had aged ten years overnight. She walked to the window. "When I first lost my daughter, she was so fragile, like a tiny, beautiful, innocent glass cup. I realized I wouldn't always be there to protect her, so I made a promise. If I ever got her back, I would do everything in my power to ensure no one could hurt her. That she could navigate life on her own. It sounds good and responsible and clever on paper but somewhere along the line I think I lost sight of the bigger picture. I often wonder what life would be like if her father staye—"

"What do you want?" Gilbert growled.

"For the moment? An ear. Emotion isn't exactly celebrated in my line of work, and even less so when you reach my position. Besides, this is as close to a funeral as she'll get."

He eased back but continued trying to loosen his hands.

"Why didn't you stop her? You were right there."

"You know, I've seen a lot of things, Mister Casanova. I've fought mercenaries, waged war, tortured, all that. I once watched a group of starving children kill and devour one of their own like a pack of rabid rats until all that was left was gnawed, clean, white bone. Never phased by any of it. But seeing my daughter bash her face into the rocks, screaming as some invisible villain drove her to madness…" She looked at him. "I don't know why I didn't stop her. Maybe I was too frightened by what I created. Maybe I wanted her to stop suffering. Maybe it was a lot of things."

There was a knock on the door.

"Mother, we need to be leaving soon," said an agent.

Silver nodded.

"I apologize for any inconvenience I've caused. You seem like a decent enough fellow. Truly. A nurse will come by in an hour and undo the restraints. Please don't harm him. On the table next to you is an envelope detailing what you are to tell the press."

Gilbert glanced at the yellow package.

"I'm giving you the treasure. All of it save one item, a pearl. As I said, the details are inside but the gist of it is you were Layla London's protege. After a freak accident on her island you made your way to Alaska and then France with the strictest orders to not say a word until the treasure was found."

"A freak accident you caused. And what about North Carolina?"

"Nothing. Believe me, you don't want to be associated with that screw up."

Fair enough. "What's to stop me from turning you in?"

"For one, no one would believe you. And in case you forgot, I still have names and addresses of people you care about. I feel guilt for my daughter, but I haven't changed. I still have a family to look after. For what it's worth, your friend seemed like a good man. His wife and children have been compensated heav—"

"Please leave."

Silver stopped talking and walked to the door and opened it. "Indulge me one last story. As I said, this is the closest thing to a funeral as she'll get. When she was a child, I'd take her to the park, and she'd run and play with the other kids. All the parents knew what I was and stayed away, but she didn't. She'd smile and laugh. The cutest, littlest laugh. I wanted to stay there all day because she was happy. And that made me happy." She cleared her throat. "I hope we never cross paths again, Mister Casanova. Good day."

She shut the door.

Part 9
One Last Thing

December 4, 2022

56 ... The Fool From Nowhere

There was thunder in the distance.

JEROME PARKER CASANOVA

JANUARY 6, 1969 - SEPTEMBER 3, 2021

LOVING FATHER, HUSBAND, AND SON

Maybe it was another Jerome Casanova? Gilbert lowered himself to the grass and stared at the gravestone. Silently he hoped he'd have trouble finding it.

Breathe.

"Took me a while, but I finally made it. You see Tennessee's doing alright? They play Georgia today. We have this really good quarterback that'll probably win the Heisman. Crazy stuff. I hear Knoxville is a mad house. Saw a video of a house catching fire because some guys burned a couch. May drive up and see people. Oh, I was out fishing the other week and caught this massive salmon. Should've seen it. Would've made all yours look like nothing."

What else?

"Saw the latest Hornet movie. It was alright, but I'm starting to agree with you. They're going downhill. Action is good, but it's all jokes and it gets kind of boring after a while. Fun stuff, though."

"I've been going on dates here and there. Shocker, right? Nothing really serious, just grabbing coffee or going for a walk. Nice girls, but…I don't know. None are really grabbing my attention. Maybe my standards are too high. This one girl, she mentioned she was looking for something long term and I was immediately like 'no'. I do want that. Eventually. But just hearing it made me feel caged. We'll get there."

The wind picked up. Hopefully the rain would hold off.

"I bought a house up in Alaska. Who would've thought I'd be a homeowner? It's a good size, right on the water. Beautiful. Quiet. The people are friendly. I think I saw an orca. Haven't given anyone the address yet."

"Swung through Detroit a couple months back and grabbed dinner with Georgia. She's doing alright. Gavin…well…even before, we never really talked, so not much has changed. And

Jake? Man. His voice dropped and it's the funniest thing." His stomach caught and the next words came out a whisper, "Mom. She's not ready. Not yet, at least."

Breathe.

"You'll get a kick out of this. Apparently, I'm an international hero. Gilbert Casanova: the man who found Womack's treasure. Folks are calling about books and movies and interviews and all that. It was fun at first. President of France gave me a medal for some reason. Had dinner at the White House. Picture in all the papers and magazines. It's weird. I was on one of those late-night shows a while back and the whole process…here's what happens. You show up, put on a bunch of makeup, then they tell you to smile. Say a few lines, tell a couple stories, and everybody ooh's and aah's." He grinned and shook his head. "Bunch of bull. Some guy said he'd give anything to experience what I did. Everywhere I go, people want to hear about the glory. The fame. The treasure. The adventure of Gilbert Casanova. Everywhere I go. Even now it doesn't feel real. Like it actually happened." He rocked on his feet and flexed his hand.

"I regret running, but I don't regret the adventure. Seeing what I've seen. Feeling what I've felt. Sometimes I wonder what it would be like if I didn't go, how different things would be. I shouldn't have gone, but I don't think I'd change it. Is that wrong?"

A car passed blasting music.

"Yeah, I thought so." He stood and laid a hand on the stone. "I'm sorry I wasn't there for you. For the family. I should've been better. And I'm not ready to forgive you, but I can't keep holding onto this anger. I want you to know I love you, and I miss you, and that you did a good job."

What now?

He looked past the gloom and death of the graveyard to the horizon where the sun was just breaking through. A smile crossed his face. "Think I might grab some pizza. Seems like a good enough place to start." Anything else? Any final words? Any last little surprises?

"See you around Jerome."

With that Gilbert let go and headed for the parking lot, his mind wandering towards the long journey home.

46 ... A Very, Very, Very, Very Long Day

Gilbert rushed to the edge. Nothing. He threw off his bag and dove.

The initial shock forced him to surface. He yelled into the night. Even if he found her they would surely freeze. He took a gulp of air and went back.

The shrivel of luck was the narrow width, but the river was deep. He could go right by without even knowing. He reached blindly, the current dragging him along. His lungs cried and legs caught fire. Again he surfaced.

They were so close to the end. What possessed her to jump? Why did he yell? All she wanted was to go back to Silver. The killer was dead. The treasure was within reach. Why throw it all away?

After an eternity, he emerged with the slack corpse and rolled it onto the rocky shore. Pale green eyes stared straight up at the night. Gilbert patted the cold cheeks. Pulse? Ribs cracked as he pushed down. One. Two. Three.

He counted to thirty, pinched the nose, and blew.

"Come on. Come on." Again he tried.

The body remained lifeless.

Heat began to swell inside Gilbert's stomach. Each compression grew more forceful until he was pounding the chest. She shuddered like jelly. Moisture filled his eyes.

The adventure would end. They would find him the next morning still pushing, still blowing, still hopelessly hoping. Angela would be thrown in some unmarked grave and he'd be taken for questioning. A connection would be made with the corpse aboard the train. He'd be tossed in a French prison. If lucky he'd live out the rest of his days in relative peace, or until Silver came to collect. Then the real hell. The torture. The mythical treasure of Womack would stay a myth. He'd be forgotten. Beside his name it would read 'coward, traitor, murderer'. What hell could he expect in the next life? Cold? Hot? Live damnit!

Warm water surged into his mouth. Angela coughed violently and gasped for air. Gilbert went numb, his knees sinking in the hard sand.

Alive, Angela Bronte buried her face in his shirt and began to cry.

47 ... Cat and Mouse

"One cheeseburger, one salad, and two chocolate milkshakes, please," said Gilbert.

The waitress, late teens he guessed, looked at him with a face that screamed 'why are you here at three in the morning and making me work?'

"Je ne vous comprends pas," she said.

It's too early for this. He pointed at the pictures on the menu. There was something amusing about finding an American themed diner in a small French town. Pink walls, checkered floor, bright red seats. Retro memorabilia and cartoons on every television. And the waitress didn't speak a word of English.

He looked at Angela. Her face was pale and dead and her eyes stayed locked on a screen.

"We might be able to squeeze in a little sleep before the train."

No reply.

"Never really watched TV as a kid. You?"

The waitress returned with the food. Gilbert took one bite and the awful mixture of grease, meat, and processed cheese cannon-balled straight to his stomach. He already felt the fat clogging his veins and contemplated whether or not to hold the pressure building in his lower intestine.

"What's the worst thing you've ever eaten?"

She laughed at the cartoon cat chasing a mouse.

"Are your clothes still wet?" He tried a number of other questions.

"This the one with the spinach guy, right?"

Her eyes shifted from the television to him.

He shrugged.

"I used ta watch when I was younger. Every Saturday mama and I would get up real early and gather all the pillows and blankets and make this huge fort and we'd watch and eat this big bowl of cereal without milk. Always without milk. I'd steal the marshmallows when she wasn't looking. After that she'd take me ta the park and I'd get ta play with the other kids. I- We- We stopped when we moved, ya know. We stopped a lotta things." She started picking her nails. "Ya know, sometimes I wonder what happened ta 'em. What those kids are up ta now. If they got ta go ta school, ta sports, ta all that boring stuff. And sometimes I wonder what it'd be like ta be 'em, ya know."

"Angela..."

"Mama changed. She says things are better but I- I don't know anymore, ya know. She's always been right."

A thought occurred to Gilbert. "You knew that man, didn't you? On the train?"

"His name was Dillon."

"One of Silver's?"

"Yeah."

"Did you know they'd be in Paris?"

"I- Maybe. Yes. Mama was tired of waiting."

"For the treasure?"

"For ya ta die."

Lovely. Gilbert poked at his hamburger, a weak smile crossing his face. He pictured the exchange between Madame Silver and her followers, the annoyance that trained professionals couldn't kill the great Gilbert Casanova. Then there was the matter of Angela. Surely she'd been tasked to kill him as well. Was the display back in Paris just an act, or had things between them actually started to thaw? Yes, he had feelings, but he did for most women who talked to him. He closed his eyes and mapped out the different possibilities.

"Gilbert?" Angela drew him back. "Why'd ya do this? Why'd ya give up the quiet life?"

He turned the question over in his mind. "Different reasons. Boredom. Glory. Impulsiveness. Sometimes, I don't know, sometimes I just want to fade away. Forget everything, and everything forget me. I don't know if that makes sense, but something about that feels easier. Romantic, even. All the mistakes, the disappoints, the expectations, all that, just gone. Like a blank canvas that only I can screw up. And I don't want to be a burden to anyone else anymore. And even though I love my friends, my family, I hate watching them grow old and waste away. I hate watching, knowing I can't do anything to stop it."

"So ya ran from it all?"

"There's more to it, but yeah. Guess I did."

"Did ya ever expect ta find the treasure?"

"Sometimes. I don't know. Sometimes I hope something would happen and that'd be it."

The silence carried for a time.

"I get that."

"Get what?"

"The sometimes. I don't...I don't always. Just sometimes." She shifted in her seat. "These voices...they're always talking.

Always whispering. Telling me, reminding me. It's been almost a year and, and I'm scared," her eyes fell, "I'm scared of what next week looks like. Next month. Next year. I'm scared of being fifty, sixty, seventy, still rolling in my own piss. Still screaming at someone not there. And part of me knows I can't go home. That no matter what, I'll never make another fort with mama, or go ta the park, or…" Blood streamed from under her nails. "I want ta be Angela. Just Angela."

He closed then opened then closed his mouth. There were a million things he wanted to say, but at the moment silence seemed the best.

Gilbert got out of his chair, walked around the table, and sat down next to her. Angela flinched when he took her hands in his.

48 ... Peace at Last

With a screech the train stopped at the crumbling station. Angela and Gilbert were the only ones to depart.

The town was dead. No cars, no dogs, no people. An old brick wall hid any view of homes. Even though Paris was cold, the lively atmosphere made it bearable. This...this was just bitter. He dug his chin into his scarf and followed the cobblestone until it merged with asphalt.

The brownish green hills of the French countryside rolled to a milky white. He was impressed by the old stone houses and the tall yet expertly manicured hedges and the painted windows and the dark roofs. Even more interesting were those that sat barren.

There was a certain charm in the run-down fences and wandering livestock.

Eventually a small brown-red cottage came into view. Four horses, their winter coats covered with a light dusting, grazed in a field. Adjacent was a discolored old barn with equipment laying out front.

"Casa-no-va!" A dark man in a simple navy sweater waved frantically from an open window. "Door's unlocked!"

Angela whistled. "Hey. What're we walking in ta?"

"He's a good man. Comes on a little strong, though."

John was already standing outside with arms and fingers stretched. The two men embraced.

"It is so, so, so good to see you! Hold on, gotta make ya pop." John squeezed tightly and made a popping noise. "And you must be Angela!" Her outstretched hand collapsed against her chest as John threw his arms around her. Gilbert had never seen someone so uncomfortable. "I've heard so much about you. I absolutely love your hat."

She squirmed free. "Are the horses ready? Are the bags packed?"

"Yes! But I've got some lunch for y'all first. Been wanting to catch up with this one for a while." Gilbert winced as John grabbed his shoulder. "Y'all are in rough shape. Come inside, I'll get the first aid kit while y'all rest."

Unpacked boxes and musical instruments were haphazardly tossed about. Pictures of family and friends lined the walls, and above the kitchen window were the words *Love Your Neighbor as Yourself*. Gilbert recognized most of the matching furniture, but the bright interior looked recently renovated. Two green duffle bags filled with food and supplies sat on the counter along with three large sandwiches.

"Are ya any good at stitching?" Angela pulled up her sleeve to reveal a deep gash.

John took her arm and studied the wound. "I should be able to. Need to clean it first. Wait here." He went down the hallway.

She met Gilbert's stare. "What were ya gonna do, sow it with a shoelace and knife? I've seen ya hands shake. I like my arm."

"Here we are." John emerged with a small sowing kit. "I don't have anything to numb the area."

"I'll be fine." Her face twitched as he set to work.

"So, Angela, Gilbert tells me you're into history. I used to teach a class on musical history. Jazz, Baroque, storytelling, all of it."

She snorted. "That's not history."

He grinned. "I said the same thing when I was in college. I had this plan of becoming the next great pianist. Rockefeller Center. Sydney Opera House. My name in lights and people worshipping the ground I walked on. All that fame and glory non-sense."

"Still could," added Gilbert, "you're the best I've ever seen."

"I'm the only you've ever seen."

"Why'd ya stop?"

"Never really stopped, just priorities changed. Sometimes life throws a curve ball and you have to decide which direction you want to go. Which dreams you need to keep, which you have to hold, and which you have to let go to make room for new ones. As cliche as it sounds, this particular curve ball was a woman named Margret."

"So ya gave up just like that?"

"No. No. Of course not. I pushed for her to move with me to New York, but she wanted to stay in Tennessee. Wouldn't budge. My parents told me to call it quits and find someone else, and I was going to. I was gonna break up with her. Had the whole thing planned out. I was gonna show up at her house, tell her how great she was, and how I wasn't the man she deserved. Well, I'm getting ready to leave and I hear a knock on the door. It's Gilbert's dad. He sits me down and tells me that I'm about to make the biggest mistake of my life. Said, 'Johnny. You're crazy. This girl is perfect. What you guys have, people spend their entire lives searching for. Don't be an idiot.' And we go back and forth, back and forth, for the rest of the night. Made me miss dinner. But he was right. Later that week I went and bought a ring. Best decision I ever made. After that I took a job teaching until someone approached me about leading music at a church. Did that for several years, got involved with a few ministries, had two kids. Got a few gray hairs. Lost the rest. Never regretted it for a minute."

Angela looked confused. "Did ya ever wonder what if ya did different?"

"I did for the first year or so, but eventually I moved on. Sometimes we get it right. Sometimes we get it wrong. Mostly we make it up and just hope." He stood up. "And that should do it. May want to go see an actual doctor. Now," he turned to Gilbert. "There's some boxes out in the barn I need help moving."

49 ... The Marathon Man

Gilbert breathed it all in: piles of green manure, armies of feasting horse flies, puddles of yellow-rotted wood, a pyramid of hay bales in the back. A questionable ladder climbed to a second floor.

"Yeah," said John, "it's not much, but we'll get there. I'm thinking of adding a row of lights and probably a workbench right along that wall."

"Like it. Maybe some new stalls. Couple benches. How's upstairs?"

"Right now, it's just storage. Margret wants to turn it into a little bed and breakfast. Rent it out."

"Don't seem too excited."

"Most people wouldn't like waking up to the smell. But if she wants it, I'll do it."

"I'll be sure to visit."

"Yeah? Figured you'd just go sleep with the horses. Make you a spot right next to Hemingway." He leaned against Gilbert and laughed.

"Maybe. What'd you need help with?"

"Why don't you grab that chair."

Gilbert's stomach twisted. He knew what was coming.

John sat across and began cleaning his boot with a knife. "Doing alright? You look tired."

He felt like death. "I'll manage. You? Margaret?"

"She's good, she's good. Not much happens when you reach our age. Tell me about this girl. She seems a little rough, but nice."

"She's something. Different, but in a good way, I think."

"Y'all dating?"

"No."

"Do you want to be?"

"Eh. I'm not sure. She's…she's got a lot of things to work through."

"Seems like you have that in common."

Gilbert flinched. "Can we not?"

"Gilbert."

"I'm fine."

"Gilbert."

"We really need to get going."

"Gilbert."

His hands started to shake. "I've got nothing to say about it. What's done is done."

"Your brother called a couple weeks ago. He...You know how he gets. Reminds me of your dad."

"Don't." He eyed the door. "How's mom? She alright?"

"She's hanging in there. She misses her son. Gavin, Jake, Georgia, they won't say it, but they miss their brother. If you just went home and apologized, I'm sure they'd forgive you."

"Why?"

"Because they're your family."

"Not that. Why should I apologize? Why me? Why am I the bad guy in all this? I'm not the one who quit."

"Your dad didn't quit. Don't come in here saying stuff like that."

"Yeah he did. He quit on you. He quit on mom. On Gavin. On Georgia. On Jake. On me. He was my best friend. And- And one day he just decides 'welp, that's it'?"

"And what did you do? Your family needed you and you ran. You go missing for months, only telling a few people that you're in South America. Then you call me up asking to get all this stuff, and you show up all bloody with this strange girl. This isn't you."

"Maybe it is. Maybe this is who I am. But I didn't quit. I've been down that road. I've been in that pit, in that- that- that darkness. And I didn't quit. I never quit because I could look at him, I could look and know if he could keep going, so could I. And now... It was selfish. Cowardly. He took the easy way."

"You talk like he did nothing. He raised your brothers. He raised your sister. He raised you. He kept a roof over y'all's heads and food on the table. He put y'all through school. He was good to your mom. And he always tried to do right. Yes, he was hard on y'all, but he loved his kids more than anything. When you finally have children, you might start to understand."

"He was never there. He was always working. He worked and worked and worked. We'd be at dinner and the phone would ring, or something made him stay late at the office. And he'd come home too tired to do anything else. He'd just sit there on the computer, and mom would tell us to leave him alone. I hated him for it. I saw him maybe two hours a day growing up, even less in college, and now, well," he forced a smile, "here I am." Gilbert wiped the tears.

The day replayed in his head. The fear. The uncertainty. The embarrassment. The sudden emptiness. The feeling of drowning in the middle of a storm. The anger. At his father. At the world. At himself.

"He called me the morning it happened. He called me twice. And both times I didn't pick up. And when I got that message, saying he did what he did, I just sat there on the couch. Frozen. Staring at my phone even after the battery died. And I kept thinking, what if? What if I'd just answered? If I'd just stepped outside for a minute? If I'd told him just how much he meant to me. To everyone. I- I don't think he would've done it. I think he would've still been around, and he would've talked me out of going on this whole stupid adventure. All the people…all the families…John…it's all my fault. I wish I would've told him he was a good man. A good dad."

"It's not your fault. You didn't know. He never liked to talk about it, but his own dad wasn't around much. It was something he struggled with, something he was scared of. Jerome was by no means perfect. I can't tell you how many times he said that. He'd tell me he worked too much, missed too many games, felt like he failed y'all. He was hard on himself. But he did love you." John scratched his chin and exhaled. "Gilbert, please go home. Give up this crazy fantasy before you get hurt."

As badly as he wanted to run back to his old life, Gilbert couldn't bring himself to it. It had nothing to do with Silver, or family, or Angela, or fame, or money, or anything like that. The closer he came to the treasure, the more certain he was that all his problems would be solved when he found the treasure. He was too close to give up.

Gilbert looked at John. "I can't."

Part 8
The Pirate Womack

December 31, 2021

50 ... L'or des Fous

Gilbert grunted as he fell to the ground. The tunnel was wet and dark, and strands of dead plants hung from every crevice and rock. The loud echo of footsteps was met with the intermittent dripping of water and whistle of cool air.

"Ya really need ta work on the rolls."

"I'll buy a bakery." He flicked on a light.

Arches and murals were carved into the stone. The place reminded him of a forgotten church.

"How long do you think it took to make all this place?"

"Decades? Well, here, look," Angela pointed at a drawing of men hunting deer. "These don't match anything being made during Womack's time. These are old. Centuries, even. My guess is this was once a ceremonial temple and overtime it was forgotten. Then one day someone stumbled on it, threw in their own tastes, forgot, rinse, repeat, until voila."

Gilbert ran his hand along the stone. He wondered what the person who carved it was like, what they thought, if they could imagine that one day some strangers would be talking about it.

The path twisted and dropped. They were moving fast. Too fast.

"Easy there." Angela grabbed him before he walked off a ledge. She kicked a rock into the darkness. They listened to it bounce off the contraption before them.

The structure was a masterpiece of metal and wood, reminiscent of a great clock. Rotted beams suggested a platform was once attached.

"Probably an elevator ta get everything down." A smile crossed her face. "Can ya imagine building this? And in the heart of France?"

"Think it still works?" Gilbert tapped a board with his foot.

"Nah. We're gonna have ta climb."

"Wonderful." He edged out. The platform shuddered.

"Careful."

"I know how to walk."

Minutes later he reached the main body. It was terrifying up close. The cold steel was a foot thick and looked ready to crush anything unfortunate enough to fall in. If they set it off, survival looked slim.

Each move was unbearably slow. In near blindness they crawled from beam to beam, freezing at every creak and mechanical sigh. Gilbert continuously wiped the sweat from his face and focused on anything but his aching hands. The treasure couldn't be too far, right? The machine had been dead for hundreds of years. They were good. They were good.

His foot slipped and kicked a rock free.

A thud echoed from above.

Then another.

Then another.

The structure jolted and the cave filled with booms and clicks and sparks. Metal scraped against metal. Debris plummeted past. The siren of death wailed once again. It was alive.

Gilbert dropped through the air. His jaw snapped through a thin board. As he scrambled for leverage pressure built around his foot. He fought to free himself. The limb continued to pull away. The wheels were closing in. Seconds more and he would be crushed.

Gilbert yanked his naked foot out and watched the boot vanish. "Don't get caught in between!"

"No shi—" He could hear Angela's scream above.

Massive cogs banged off the stone walls sending chunks of rock barreling by. Gilbert chanced a look above. The entire ceiling was bathed in orange.

A bloody hand covered his mouth. "On three we jump!"

"Wait, Angela!"

"Three!"

They smacked into the shattered ground and crawled to a sheltered hole. Debris continued raining down.

After five minutes the cave grew quiet and they continued.

51 ... Traps, Traps, and More Traps

"Stop," said Angela. "Something doesn't feel right."

Bright light penetrated the vines.

"I don't see anything."

"Cause ya an idiot." She reached into her bag and pulled out a tennis ball. "Watch." She threw it into the light.

Clang!

A row of rusted spikes shot from the ceiling carrying two partially decomposed bodies. They slowly sunk back into their holes. Her breathing quickened.

"Guess we're not the first to find this place. You good?"

"Y- Yeah. Just follow me."

The tunnel narrowed the further they went.

"How's this compare to other gigs?"

"This place or the adventure as a whole?"

"As a whole."

"Eh. Less killing. Kind of nice ta work with someone for a change. Definitely not the smoothest operation."

"Think you may stick with it?"

"Yeah, maybe."

"You don't have to."

"And what, run off with ya?"

He wasn't going to say it quite like that. "Is that the worst thing?"

"Gilby…shut up and focus."

Skeletons carpeted the floor, squashed flat.

His eyes traveled up. There was the slightest separation between wall and roof.

"The—"

"I see it."

Angela brought out a wire and shaped it into a hook. She wrapped it around the end of a stick and, from a distance, pulled on a vine.

Thwack!

A portion of the ceiling slammed the ground.

"Don't touch anything."

Bones crunched and snapped.

Deeper they went. Gilbert forgot about his injuries and his exhausted state. He could fell the excitement. He could taste the gold.

Again, Angela stopped him.

Nothing seemed out of place. There were no bodies. Gilbert took a step then froze. There were no bodies.

"The floor."

"Yeah."

Angela stretched her foot out, easing it onto the stone. Nothing. She brought the next forward.

Whoosh!

Her leg shot through the ground and the floor vibrated. Webs. Gilbert pulled her up.

"There's no floor."

"No shit Sherlock."

Gilbert picked up a stone and tossed it. He listened, but never heard it hit the bottom.

Angela studied the wall. She pushed back vines to reveal a square cutout.

"Keys."

He handed her the pieces.

She snapped them together and pushed it into the spot. A low groan filled the tunnel. Walls shook, vines snapped, and a thick slab of stone scraped across the chasm. Halfway across there was a cry and it stopped moving.

When they reached the other side he spotted a corpse laying against a wall. There was a letter in its hand.

To whoever reads this, know that I, Edmond Brown, was betrayed by Louis Frank. The man has gone mad. He kills any who question him. He promises riches beyond our dreams but works us until we collapse. No treasure is worth death. I was preparing to leave and the bastard shot me in the back. I called for mutiny, but the rest have followed him. My time is short. My sight fades. If you have come searching for this awful prize, abandon it before it claims you as well.

Deeper they went.

"Smell that?"

Gilbert inhaled. He detected the faintest traces of spice…and oil?

"We're close."

The tunnel expanded into a large room. In the center was an ancient altar. Beyond that was a large metal door. Hundreds of golden vines were intricately carved into the surface, each leading to the ground. At the base were bones and cloth. Gilbert felt the fine details. This was it. This was the last great myth. The fortune of a thousand sailors. The treasure of the Pirate Womack.

His eyes focused on the bodies. He knelt and used his gun to search. Something wasn't right. There were multiple thin cuts, as if it were stabbed. A piece of paper rolled to the floor.

The captain has lost his mind. We are without food. We are without men. I begged him we leave to gather more supplies and the man laughed. Laughed! He said the treasure is here, the pearl is inside, that we are so close, that if we leave now some-one else will come along. I continued my case. Even if we get the door open, then what? We are too few. The captain gave me one of his looks, told me to take heart, to not cause chaos. His intentions were clear as blood. I said I was just tired and rest would serve me well.

Let them rot. All of them. If they want to die for this treasure, so be it. I will not wait around. I leave tonight.

Zang!

Gilbert's soul left his body and he checked if he'd been hit. Angela's laughter echoed in the darkness, along with the terrible scrapping of metal on stone.

Zang!

"Can you not?"

"One of these opens the door. Trial and error, baby."

Zang!

He took a closer look at the wall. Dozens of fist sized holes were connected by the vines.

For over an hour they took turns, the awful cry ringing in his ears. Gilbert contemplated throwing himself in their way, if only to escape the noise.

A vein pulsed on Angela's head. "This is taking too long!" She jammed the tool into a new hole and struggled to pull it out. A crack filled the air and the stick splintered into a thousand pieces. "No no no!" She threw the remains at the wall and began cursing in Spanish.

The outburst surprised him.

"No I'm not good! We don't have time. They're almost here. The stick just broke."

"Who's almost here?"

Her breathing slowed and she regained her composure. "No one. No one's here. I'm just tired. That's all. We've been followed so far and…I'm just tired."

Gilbert decided to leave it at that and return to the wall. Maybe they could find another stick? Or a marking? A hint? Anything? There had to be an answer. An answer? Gilbert took off his pack and pulled out the keys. "Let me see your light."

Angela handed it over. "Ya not gonna find anything without the phrase."

He wasn't convinced. "Layla thought the keys were important. Even you said we had to have them." Gilbert placed the key on the altar. "What if the answer," he shined the light, "is right here?" The golden letters painted the wall.

EEHEEOEPCESTIWALISACIEOE

NIWSVTLEAHIRRAERTNHELHDR

EMDTKENSUNROTEYEFYSDEBOE

AFOORANLNWWWEUITBUMANOAT

WYFYDMESROOTHRLTEOTSATPR

BDNAEMASTKCNHCABIFINLMTVE

RRRUODDEBTNOPNVEUIYRCTNH

Angela took a seat. "Ya wasting time."

"I'm open to suggestions." Gilbert stared at the markings. What if he…no. Maybe? Not that. What about? Think. His eyes widened. Could it really be that easy? He took out his journal. His head snapped from page to wall, page to wall.

BDNAEMASTKCNHCABIFINLMTVE

EMDTKENSUNROTEYEFYSDEBOE

WYFYDMESROOTHRLTEOTSATPR

AFOORANLNWWWEUITBUMANOAT

RRRUODDEBTNOPNVEUIYRCTNH

NIWSVTLEAHIRRAERTNHELHDR

EEHEEOEPCESTIWALISACIEOE

He rearranged them again.

BEWARNE, DMYFRIE, NDFORWH, ATYOUSE, EKDROVE, MEMADTO, ANENDLE, SSSLEEP, TURNBAC, KNOWTHE, CROWNIS, NOTWORT, HTHEPRI, CERUNAW, AYLIVEA, BETTERL, IFEBUTI, FYOUINS, ISTMYHA, NDSAREC, LEAN-CLI, MBTOTHE, TOPANDO, VERTHRE, E

Gilbert made a final pass and read what he saw.

"Be warned my friend for what you seek drove me mad to an endless sleep turn back now the crown is not worth the price run away live a better life but if you insist my hands are clean climb to the top and over three."

A rhyme? Really? He half expected the room to start shaking and a magical door to appear.

Angela dropped her head. "I hate ya, ya know."

"It's my best quality." He approached the wall and climbed. Layers of dust and webs stuck to his fingers. He reached in.

"Ya at the wrong one. Climb ta the top and over three. Three from the right."

Gilbert hesitated. Where did the numbers start? Was this another puzzle?

"Are you sure?" Who counts from the right?

No answer.

Who counts from the right? Gilbert stared at the holes trying to decide. No pressure, right? One leads to the greatest treasure in history, the other impalement by rusty spikes. He went with his gut and stayed. He could feel creatures crawling up his arm.

"Please be right." He grabbed the rope and yanked.

Deep within the walls rose a mechanical rumble. The volume steadily increased. Damn! He must've grabbed the wrong one. The place was about to collapse. With a groan, the door parted, and the tunnel fell silent.

52 ... Womack's Treasure

The room erupted in a fiery light that painted the walls with every color imaginable and shimmered off mountains and mountains of treasure.

Ruby reds. Sapphire blues. Emerald greens. Pink diamonds. Black opals. Thick, thick cobwebs covered thousands of gold coins and silver chains from all corners of the earth. Spanish. English. Chinese. French. Indian. Expertly crafted chests held spices that stung the nose and made his eyes water. Pallet after pallet of exotic woods — purples, ambers, stripes — supported the most elegant rugs and curtains and furs he'd ever seen. Golden roses with soft pink linings. Panthers and bears and whales. Family crests. Stories lost to history.

Beautiful, gorgeous paintings of oil hung with the faces of men and women long dead, the sickly-sweet smells still lingering in the air. Jeweled statues sat at attention in small alcoves continuing their guard. Gilbert dug a hand into a pile of gold and watched the cold metal slip through his fingers and scatter across the floor.

Holy shit.

"We did it!" Angela tackled him to the ground, laughing. She ran through the room touching every surface and opening every box.

He sat back. "We did it." The words felt foreign. A dream that was impossible. Gilbert Casanova found the treasure of the Pirate Womack. Gilbert Casanova found the treasure of the Pirate Womack. Gilbert Casanova found the treasure of… Tears filled his eyes.

"This is from the Ming dynasty," Angela dropped the piece and moved to another, "That's Egyptian. This must've been Babylonian. I used ta collect emeralds just like this for a necklace. That has ta be Indian. Look at all this!"

Gilbert's attention was drawn to a skeleton leaning against a far column. Underneath tired layers of cloth, patches of gray skin clung to the bones. He called Angela over.

She appeared besides him decked out in colorful robes and golden jewelry. "Bow before ya queen."

He grinned. "Maybe one day. Think that's Womack?"

She removed her headdress and stooped next to the body. She explored the clothes and pulled out a long sheet and shiny pearl. Falling back on a pile of silver she began to read. "Here lies the Pirate Daniel Womack…twenty-thousand pounds of gold…thirty of silver…lots of jewels…yadda yadda yadda…some paintings. It's a manifest."

"Anything personal?"

"Nah."

Gilbert took the list and read it himself. There were enough riches to last a million lifetimes. He rolled the pearl in his hand. There was something strange about it. As if it were alive. He placed both the document and rock in his pocket.

"Ya alright? Thought ya'd be more excited."

"Yeah, no. It's nothing. It's just…I don't know. I thought after all this, after finding the treasure, I'd be…happy? Satisfied? Instead I just feel empty." He looked around the room. "Meet you back by the bridge. Need a few minutes." He waited until he no longer heard footsteps.

Gilbert picked up a jeweled cup and looked at his reflection. He hardly recognized the creature. "You found the freaking treasure." He chucked it across the room and listened to it clatter along. What was supposed to happen? Fireworks? Superpowers? Everything to make sense? When he first set out, he had no idea what to expect. Everything was new and each day was an adventure. It was exciting. He had a purpose and that purpose drove every decision. Now what? There was no great realization, no metamorphosis, no nothing. Just rocks and metal and cloth. Life continued. Silver would come and take the treasure and he'd grow old and die and his name forgotten. The only difference between him and the dead captain was Gilbert currently lived. He went through hell and had nothing to show for it except for a few scars and two less fingers. "You're a goddamn idiot, Gil."

Exhaustion rolled over him. First sleep. After that? He'd figure it out later. And what about Angela? Sure there were a lot of red flags...a lot...but still...

"Hey Angela, do you have anything going on later?" No. "Hey, An-ge-la." God, that's bad. Coffee? He didn't drink coffee. Did she? Why was this so hard? Just act natural. "Hey Angela, do you like pizza?" He continued down the tunnel trying to craft the perfect sentence. Worst she could say is no, right?

Up ahead he heard voices. He slowed and listened.

"Mama it's all down there. Just—"

"Shut up. What do you mean he's not yet dead?

53 ... The Walls of Jericho

"Hello dears." Madame Silver stood near the bridge with John. "I tried calling but the reception must be awful."

Gilbert's hand shot to his side.

"Please wait to grab your weapon until you are ready to die. We can still be civilized."

"Why is he here?" said Gilbert. "We found the treasure."

"And you did such a wonderful job. Four killed in Paris. Thousands in damages. A whole coverup on the train. And must I remind you, we made a deal. You had one month to find the treasure and, well, one month came and went, oh," she looked at her wrist, "two hours and twenty-three minutes ago. And you," she turned to Angela, "you were supposed to kill him. Again, you fail me."

"Mama. I- We- The treasure is right down there. Let them go."

"I would love to, but," a smile crossed her face, "know what? It's the Christmas season and I'm in a giving mood. Jericho," Angela straightened, "you have the honors. Choose."

Jericho? Gilbert looked from Angela to Silver. His mind processed the information. Angela J. Bronte. His eyes widened. It all made sense.

"N- No."

"No? I must have misheard you." Silver spoke slowly, softly, making sure each syllable of every word was understood in its entirety. "I offered you two choices, and you chose this one. Now you have one last choice to make. It's easy enough. Even for you. You have a gun. You have two targets. Now choose."

"Angela?" John's voice broke. "Please. Walk away."

"Finish this, and everything goes back to normal. We can be a family again."

"Don't listen to her!" Gilbert shouted, "Angela!"

"You have five seconds to fire that gun or I will put a bullet in this man. Then I will wait until every last coin, every last necklace, every last bit of treasure is emptied out of this place and then put a bullet in your friend's head and leave the body to rot. Five."

"Wait! We found the treasure!" Gilbert rushed forward but was grabbed by two men. They found the treasure. They found it.

"Four."

"Stop!" Please. Please!

"Three."

"Mama?" said Angela

"Tw- Two."

Oh god. "John!"

"One."

Bang!

John's shirt darkened around the chest and quickly spread to the waist. He coughed blood and fell back. "Gilbert?"

"No!" Gilbert broke free and ran to his friend. "John? John? No no no."

The tense appearance faded and the body went slack.

Silver walked up to Angela and took her by the jaw and rubbed her cheek. "Oh daughter. You were almost perfect."

"Mama?" Angela's voice cracked. "Mama? Where are ya going? What about me?"

"You? What about you? You failed. Again. After everything I did for you, you couldn't do the simplest task." She threw Angela's head. "What about you? What kind of a question is that?

Time after time you let me down. I gave you all I could. I should've listened to everyone. What about you? You get to live. And if I ever catch so much as a whiff of your scent, I won't send another grunt. I brought you into this world screaming. I can rip you out just the same."

Gilbert closed John's eyes and charged Silver. Right before reaching her, he was hit from the side and sent over the edge onto the bridge.

The structure groaned. Gilbert wiped the blood from his mouth and looked up. Silver's lips curled with cruel pride as Angela stared him down.

He grabbed a nearby bone. "Don't do this." He swung as a warning. His ears started to ring. "Angela?"

He dodged a black shoe and swung again. The weapon splintered against her hip.

Gilbert's back screamed as he pushed under the added weight. One foot came up. Now the other. Rough hands groped his face and tore at his hair. With a cry both crashed to the floor. Boards broke and fell into the raging waters.

They struggled. Angela managed to wrap her legs around his torso and squeezed. He screamed as his insides were crushed.

"Angela! Stop!" He couldn't breathe. He was going.

Gilbert felt a jagged board and plunged the weapon into her leg and twisted. Angela let loose an animalistic howl as her knee ripped apart.

The bridge continued to fall apart. Any second the whole thing would collapse. "Stop. Please. Let's just leave."

Pain snaked up his leg as the wood slammed into his bare foot and pinned him to the ground. The starved animal pounced, digging her fingers into his throat.

He kicked while shielding himself. Come on, come on! Gilbert let out a short cry as Angela yanked the weapon free and slung him to the ground. A board broke across his face.

Gilbert was brought to his knees. He could feel a wire cutting into his neck.

Angela spat in his ear. "Stop fighting." She pulled tighter.

"Ang- Angela. Please."

Gilbert thrashed about. The taste of blood filled his mouth. His hands slapped wildly against his friend. In a desperate attempt he threw his full weight against her bad knee.

Angela staggered and fell through a hole. As she reached for support the entire structure wailed and the bearings cracked. They started to spin.

Wood and rocks rained below. The entire floor slid. Gilbert crawled for the ledge. A short scream sounded as they collided with the wall. He was nearly there. Shards ate into his hands. Boards fell. He rose higher and higher. He could make it.

"Mama! Help!"

The cries and grunts and screams nearly made him vomit.

Silver was nowhere to be seen.

Don't look. Don't look. Don't look.

He looked back.

God damnit.

Gilbert slid down to Angela and began chipping away.

The bridge was nearly vertical.

"You got to help me. I can't get you out."

"I'm trying!"

The wood slammed into the ledge and the rock collapsed sending everyone into the river below.

54 ... Ophelia

Gilbert's stomach slammed against his spine as he plunged beneath the frigid surface. He could feel himself picking up speed.

Twisting and turning through the water in violent corkscrews he began to lose vision. Arms and legs banged against rocks. Skin was split open on the jagged bottom.

His lungs caught fire. Gilbert clawed for air. Which way was up? For a split second he emerged, just long enough to steal a breath before he was sucked back under.

The world seemed to go between pitch black and a murky white.

Gilbert exploded to the surface. The raw air shredded his throat and a thin layer of ice formed across his face. He grabbed a piece of debris and dug his fingers, letting the river decide his course. For the moment, his entire existence revolved around the dark wood.

Minutes passed before he could think clearly.

On all sides were a thick layer of snow. Pockets of trees dotted the landscape. He tried to look back, but pain forced him to abandon the endeavor.

When he could finally feel the bottom he let go, straining to drag himself across the rocks and into snow. He hissed through clenched teeth at the initial shock until it faded to numbness.

How bad was the damage? He combed his senses. The still pulsing foot he already knew would need attention. His shins hurt, but mostly from the cold and overall wear. Same for the arms and hands — general bruising and cuts. Legs banged up, not broken. His chest and head felt as if someone had done a dance. His throat…damn his throat. Gilbert hoped it would all go away and not leave any lasting issues. The taste of blood remained, as did the swirling sky. And the ringing. His mind wandered to Angela.

He could hear her screaming over a hill.

He flipped over and clawed his way to the noise.

"No. No! I don't wanna go!"

As he came over the hill, he saw Madame Silver standing over a bloody and convulsing Angela.

"It's okay," he called out. His voice was nearly gone. "It's okay." He let his body roll down the rocks.

"No! Stay back!" She began to kick. A foot nailed his face. He could feel the warm liquid flow along and off his chin.

"Angela. Please." He kept crawling.

The spasms grew more intense. Blood ran down her arms, down her forehead. Gilbert was certain she'd tear her ears off.

"I don't wanna go!"

Silver stood, frozen, her face pale and warped with fear.

Gilbert's leg screamed. His back cramped. "It's me, Angela. It's your friend. Please."

He reached out and wrapped himself around her ankles.

The shrieking and shaking slowed. Angela looked at him. Red eyes, wild hair, the overall appearance of a lost devil or scared child. Her mouth moved but no words came out.

"It's okay. It'll pass. It'll pass."

"No. No it won't."

"It will."

"Gilby, I can't. I- I- ca—." She let out a horrible scream. "Get out of my head!" She reached for her leg.

"No! Angela!"

Her arm jerked and there was a flash and smoke and suddenly Gilbert couldn't hear and the sky started to rain red. The body slumped.

ABOUT THE AUTHOR

Colin O'Brien is an engineer, photographer, and writer. After graduating college from the University of Tennessee – Knoxville, he grew bored with the daily routine and joked to a friend about backpacking through Alaska. Three weeks later they were in Denali National Park battling frostbite and running from wolves. From there his love for travel took off.

Some of his adventures include herding alpacas in Peru, walking across Ireland, and working as a cowboy in the Western United States. When he's not traveling, Colin enjoys playing guitar and hiking in the Smokey Mountains.

His only goals as a writer are to be honest about both the beauty and hardships of adventure, and hopefully inspire others to go on one themselves.